W O M E N

PERFECT WE ARE NOT

STRONG WE ARE

Nicholson & Fisher

Maryland

Nicholson & Fisher Publishing

Baltimore, Maryland

Editors by
Kendra Grace, James McDonald Jr., Heather Tate
Cover Art and Design by Renee McDonald

This book is dedicated to all the mothers, daughters, sisters and wives who've doubted their strength at some point in life.

Table of Contents

Preference

Women, how do they put up with so much drama, so many crises, so much crap and still walk away with a smile and happy, or do they? That's what women want you to believe, but deep down they hurt inside just like any man or child. Women have a way of keeping it all together while struggling inside.

A Long Way Home

by
Maxine Wanda Day Camper

Mom buttoned up her coat across her chest as tears streamed down. She waved frantically. Her twenty-one-year-old daughter would learn life's lessons the hard way. "All aboard". The train screeched slowly down the track bound for Charleston, South Carolina. Let's Get Away, by Earth Wind and Fire, played as the train was leaving out of Baltimore. "I 'm grown" Carina whispered. Her chest swelled up and down until sleep over came her. Frightening trees covered in Spanish moss dotted the road to the courthouse.

"Carina Delaney do you take this man Damien Gibson as your lawful wedded husband?" I do. "I now pronounce you man and wife. You may kiss the bride."

Three months later Carina knelt cowering and confused. Her petite frame pulsating in pain as the wind exercised the Spanish moss through the picture window. The sparsely furnished immaculate one-bedroom apartment did not bear witness to her presence. A pistol bobbed up and down at her forehead. The same small black and silver pistol that lived under Damien's pillow. The clues were hidden or blindly overlooked that preceded the moment. The first week was magical. Damien would laugh, serenade and blow his Sax. He was a super star with the voice of Philip Bailey of Earth, Wind and Fire. He would lick and bite his bottom full lip. His dark brown eyes penetrating through my thoughts.

The honeymoon was spent in the bedroom. The air was thick with every area orchestrated for pleasure. The intimacy was insatiable, and time out was only used to eat and go back. Eat and go back. Eat and go back for seven days. His short afro and peach fuzz mustache glistened as his smile widened with sensual gratification. The bed squealed and moaned for relief. Damien did not take calls and only answered the door for takeout. The world remained silent outside their bedroom. Carina felt restrained under his control while the pregnant branches of the Spanish moss tree brushed quickly against their open bedroom window.

The second week Damien reported for duty to the Naval base. His tall lean, tight muscular frame in uniform made Carina's mind revert to Fort Meade as a child. Her Dad played the tuba in the 1st Army National Marching band. "Carina are you listening? said Damien with a prickly tone. Listen up, I am not going to say this again, do not open the front door and do not talk to the neighbors" his voice rising as the Emotions, Don't Ask My Neighbor, played in the background. That same day came a knock. "Is Damien home? " Asked a girl around Carina's age. She mentioned she was just returning home from college, then looked at Carina sideways. "He's on the naval base at work." Her expression soured as she made a quick turn down the stairs.

That week Damien asked what she was doing during the day. He started to curse and fuss. "There are no pigs that live here so why do you keep this place like a pigsty? She looked around and silently wondered if they were in the same apartment. I thought he would be pleased. "EVERYTHING HAS TO BE IN IT'S PLACE, DO YOU HEAR ME?" his voice roared, rising louder and still louder. He glanced under the sofa and found dust. The sofa would need to be swept under every day. He ran his middle finger across the unsteady round coffee table. The furniture needed to be dusted and polished every day. He swung open the worn kitchen cabinets one by one and pulled out the dishes. Everything inside the cabinets need to be removed once per week and the cabinets wiped down inside. Damien had a regimen of bizarre duties. She listened with agitation as her mind soon realized his fanatical obsession with cleaning. There was only one explanation for it. This dude is a NEAT FREAK.

The third week she met a young married couple through Damien. Damien would pick all her friends. She loved her some Ronnie and Debora. Debora had a big laugh and quick sense of humor by way of Pensacola Florida. Men would say she was corn bread fed. Carina could always count on Debora to cheer her up and we soon became quick road dogs. They would take drives in the countryside to see where the locals lived. She was Carina's personal tour guide and friend. Debora would point out the moon shiners and they would howl with laughter.

Any place Carina needed to go she would take her. She explained to her that whatever you do. "Carina do not mess with women from South Carolina.", Carina asked "Why?", and she said jokingly, they are Geechee and will cut you, cut you." We both rolled with laughter.

Damien was back and it was time to go to Piggly Wiggly. There was no car, so they had to walk. The road was long and drank in the dust. The sun felt hotter than ever before. The people walking wore the sun on their skin. Walking ahead and almost dragging a heavy bag in each hand Carina happened to look up as a 1978 Monte Carlo passed by. Carina turned back to see a look of disgust. A split second through the door the profanity started. A black belt, Damien did not strike her but wrestled and tossed her from the front to the back of the living room. He then put her in a choke hold and threw her on the sofa. "I saw you look at that man. Do not, do not deny it. Why would you be so stupid Carina? You wanted that man, didn't you? You slut! You tramp! You whore! " The words sounded under water as she thought of home.

The fourth week I looked up and there was a woman outside the wooden screen door. Damien introduced Carina to Jackie. Her small slanted eyes looked down at Carina. She had caused a scandal in her native Baltimore. The secret affair with her stepbrother had produced twin boys. Not able to handle the families verbal assaults they both relocated to Charleston and married. Jackie had thick lips covered in bright red lipstick. Gum popped after every other word. "Take a stick of double mint, "she said, as she continued to tell Carina about her husband Jerome. Her wide hips draped in a red polyester skirt two sizes too small. Jackie was tall, chatty, with a crying baby on each hip. She would often stop by to ask how Carina's day went. She became her confidant while the boys would crawl around the apartment unattended. Carina told her everything while she listened attentively as though taking notes.

Jackie regretted marrying Jerome and confided that she wanted to leave him. The relationship was precarious at best. Jerome swore he would take his life if she ever dared to leave. She was young and would often go the Enlisted Mans Club to cut loose. Damien was the local DJ there. Jackie would quickly offer to drive him to the club but needed a babysitter.

They both would turn and look at Carina.

The fifth week bored, Carina decided to poke her head out the door after Damien's rigid warning. Venturing out alone, no bombs went off, she thought. There goes that tree again. Thoughts of hangings, tortured anguished faces, unhappy times peppered her thoughts. She could not shake those feelings. Carina walked around the neighborhood just long enough to beat Damien back home.

She had seen his temper and did not want to do anything to set him off. Walking on eggshells was an easier accomplishment. Damien would never talk about his parents and family. Something was not quite right. Sitting in the bedroom rocking she thought of home. Oh, how she missed her family in Baltimore. If only she could go back. If only she had listened to her Mom. There was way too many ifs and life seemed so complicated. She even missed college, but it felt impossible and a long way to go back home. There were four words that stood in the way and made it near impossible, "I TOLD YOU SO". Carina scrambled for a recent polaroid picture from the dresser drawer. Her two beloved dogs, Prince Alexander Mocha-Kai Coco Tai-Tai Day, a mixed German shepherd and Ginger, a boxer, who she also called Lisa Lynn and Our Lady Margo. Carina sat and rocked with tears staring at the picture. Damien entered the bedroom and snatched the picture. Setting the picture on fire he screams, "I AM YOUR ONLY FAMILY NOW." She soon felt that her attitude of feeling grown was irresponsible and childish. She thought she was controlling her destiny, but instead delivered herself into the hands of a man that meant to control every aspect of her life.

Damien had grown up fast in Baltimore. The tragic B&O train wreak on an icy day in 1963 took part of him. Both parents now a distant memory. He was knee high when both succumbed to their tragic end. He never talked about them, but somehow it changed him inside. His young life skipped from six to eighteen. Damien joined the Navy and got out. Home on leave he met Carina and they became inseparable.

It was love at first sight. Contradiction love at first lust. She was a college student approaching her twenty-first birthday and was used to having her own way. It was a whirlwind romance. He wanted a family and she wanted a new life. Carina had made up her mind and there was no looking back. Her mother tried as she could, but to no avail, Carina would learn the hard way. Just before Carina eloped to Charleston, she met his foster parents. They were elderly and argumentative. The two-story wood frame house on Elderon street felt cold and unwelcoming with secrets she would one day know. No one talked about the temper. Damien's temper, when he was nice, he was extremely nice, but when he was mad his temperament bordered on the obscene. There was no in-between.

The sixth week although Carina hated doing laundry,

she had nothing to wear. Too many dirty clothes she thought, and her favorite tight jeans with the splits on the side could not go another day. Damien was at work so without hesitation Carina ventured out alone again. She skipped down the stairs and slid near the bottom skinning her knee, almost busting her head. She noticed the third step was now missing. Damien was obsessed with scars and would inspect her body. Carina cringed at the thought. Sorting in the laundry room someone walked up from behind and startled her.

"Hey neighbor, just moving in?" He said.

"I know who you are. I'm James and you must be Carina."

He looked excited to meet her. His face contorted and his squinty eyes danced up and down. James was dressed in baby blue double-knit pants and a paisley shirt tied at the waist. She thought him peculiar. Her large almond shaped eyes widened in disbelief as he spoke his truth. His truth went from zero to one hundred. Her mind raced on overload. How could he? Why would he? How dare he? Carina was emotionally wounded. Damien had overnight weekend duty, so Debora picked up some E&J Brandy to erase the vicious words from Carina's head. Wanting more liquor and no money, she decided to visit the Red Cross. Not knowing giving blood and alcohol did not mix she soon found out the hard way.

The weeks started to crawl by. She became home sick missing the people that she loved. I TOLD YOU SO, I TOLD

YOU SO rang in her ears. She could not understand why Damien would never give her spending money but did not want her to work. But worst of all there was no phone. She started to feel like a prisoner of war. He was always away at the Naval base or at the club. If he was not pissed off about something, they were in the bedroom exercising their favorite past time. Jackie began to stop by every day. Carina welcomed her presence. She could not hold the secret any longer. "Jackie, I just found out that Damien got James our neighbor's wife pregnant. There was a terrible fight and James got locked up.

It happened just before he came to Baltimore on leave and he KNEW. He KNEW and he let me elope down to this wretched place. He warned me not to speak to the neighbors and now I know why. They were having a steamy affair and she was in love with him.

She got an abortion out of fear from her husband. James is scary as hell. The saddest part of all is she was found hanging from a huge mossy tree in Palmetto park. Those damn trees! She took her own life when told that Damien got married. These country folks must think I'm a damn fool. She felt so dirty." Carina dissolved into tears and fell into Jackie's arms. Jackie stroked her neck and whispered, "This will pass. Everything will be just fine."

Twelve weeks had passed. The blistering summer was over. The trees covered with the squirrel tails never changed.

Their presence always made her feel uneasy. Was there a bug in the apartment? Everyone she spoke with he knew. Everywhere she went he knew. Damien was in her head. She kept a diary in the back of the bottom kitchen drawer. The drawer that Damien never opened. There her thoughts would be safe. She counted them and there were twelve pages. A page for each week. She could no longer trust the people Damien brought to the house.

He was mad most days. It was though he was reading Carina's thoughts and knew her every move. "Are you talking to the neighbors? Damien asked. "Now don't lie to me Carina." There was no need to answer. Damned if she does damned if she doesn't. She was not about to tell on herself. "Fool me once, shame on you; fool me twice shame on me." She thought. Every week Damien would try to teach her martial arts. A black belt in Taekwondo made him feel like he could throw her without showing marks. He would first push all the furniture to the sides of the walls. Then he would get in his stance, knees bent. Next, he would motion towards her and say his favorite line "come on, come at me".

Each time he would throw her over his shoulder onto the floor. Once he was satisfied with the lesson he would say, "Now get this living room back together so we can go to bed." Three months had arrived. Damien had become a popular DJ at the club. Carina was never invited, and they never went out together for enjoyment. She was his and no one could be in her presence unless they came through him. Carina was terrified of Damien and he knew it. Tried as she could to stay on his good side, she never knew when he would holler or throw her around like a ragdoll.

The first Saturday of the month and Damien was getting dressed for his gig. Jackie had already asked Carina to babysit her infant boys, that never stopped crying. She came back to the bedroom and lifted the window to let in a breeze. She told Carina that she had left her husband Jerome. "He's weak, she said. I want a real man. He's in the suicide ward of the hospital the dumb ass cut his wrist. He should have gone to Palmetto park to get the job done." The callousness in her voice and venom in her words were an abomination. Damien and Jackie soon left for the base. Carina wondered how on earth she could ever have confided in this demon. She started to think, as she rubbed her temples and laid her head in her hands. How did Damien always know what she did each day? The apartment is not bugged, but the air is rife with betrayal. Finally, the boys had fallen to sleep. A loud knock at the door, and Jackie rushes in and grabs the boys. Carina asks, "where is Damien? She says, he had to work late," and quickly rushes out. Carina walked back to the bedroom. Then she lost all consciousness. James climbed up the Spanish moss tree through the waiting window. He then dragged Carina's motionless body back into the living room.

Waking up her head is pulsating. Talking and crying

feverishly with a manic disposition James steadies a pistol up and down at Carina's swollen forehead. The same small black and silver pistol that lived under Damien's pillow. "My wife is not here because of your sorry ass. She should be here not you BITCH, he said." At that moment Damien rushed in. He had heard the commotion from outside the door. He kicked the door open with a loud bang and lunged at James. The pistol went off and the bullet missed Carina and went into the wall. Damien led with a knee to the chest and an arm down on the head. James went down to the linoleum floor hard. The police pulled into the court with the ambulance close behind.

Carina, lying in bed at Roper hospital, Damien soon arrived. He began telling her everything. "Jackie hated you" He said. On the way home she came on to me. I pushed her off and she kicked me out of her car. That's why I got home so late. I had to walk. She told me about you. She told me everywhere you went, everything you did and everyone you spoke to. Saturday night she left the window opened for James knowing his crazy ass had a vendetta against me. "Promise, just promise me Carina that you will never leave me." Damien begged.

Damien then explained that he had received orders to ship out to Italy and was leaving soon. A few days after leaving the hospital Damien was shipped to Naples, leaving Carina alone. She was happy to have time without fearing the constant abuse, though she missed Damien. Within weeks of shipping out Carina learned she was pregnant. On one hand she was excited but on the other hand she believed she would never rid herself of Damien.

After settling in Italy Damien sent for Carina. Because of the baby she was torn between joining Damien or leaving him for her sanity. She decided to join him.

Upon arriving they stayed at the Hotel Pugliesi. With paper thin walls they could hear the old sitcom Family Affair playing in the lobby while they rested in their second-floor room.

Within days the violence started again. It was rarely a day that Damien didn't use Carina as a stress reliever. The violence got worse with each beating. One day Damien pushed Carina so hard on the bathroom toilet that the seat broke in half.

Carina had enough at that point. She feared for her life and the life of her unborn child. Though she was scared of Damien's reactions she packed her bags and headed back to the states. She returned home where several days later she lost the baby.

When Damien heard of the miscarriage, he received permission to return to the states to be with Carina. She didn't really want to see him but he convinced her that things would be different.

Over the next few weeks Carina watched Damien's every move. When he was in her presence, she could only see an ugly dirty man. Day after day she waited for his shit to start again. Finally, on a beautiful Fall day the arguments started again. Standing in her third-floor bedroom they got into an argument. By that time she was done, so she told him that she wanted a divorce. They argued into the night over the divorce.

A left knee to the chest and a right arm to the head followed before Damien left, never to return again. Carina never saw Damien after that night. He disappeared with never a word sent, just a signature on a piece of paper. The marriage traumatized Carina, taking her nine years to trust again.

It was a long way home for Carina. Though she was in fear of returning to the family she missed so much Carina made her way back to them. She worried the entire trip home; afraid of the ridicules, the rejections and the "I told you so's.". But to her surprise she was greeted with tears of joy and hugs of love.

Carina married some nine years later, but this time to a loving and caring family man. The wedding was held at the New Psalmist Baptist church chapel in Baltimore. The couple was surrounded by a host of family and friends for life. At times she looks back at the mistakes that led to her marriage to Damien, but she knew she had grown.

She Once Knew My Name

by
R.C. McDonald

She was my best friend; she was the person I spent most of my time with, she was my mother. Losing her was difficult. Though her heart still beat her mind had cease.

Having been diagnose with Dementia some years prior I had plenty of time to adjust to the mental and behavioral changes expected with the disease. But adjustments were hard, they were sometimes sudden and came without warning. Some were predictable but most challenged my every strength.

Having grown up with a mother who took on any challenge with determination and authority it was hard seeing that invisible monster take the person I loved so much. Mom lived through the disappearance of her mom, the dissolution of a marriage to the man she loved more than any man and the death of a son she worried about the most. Though those low points challenged her mental strength she managed to persevere, being there for myself and my brothers.

We didn't have much money, dad worked as a teacher and Mom stayed home with us kids. Mom was trained as a Nurse but decided to stay home when my oldest brother was born.

She did her best to make sure we had what we needed. I remember Mom scrubbing the floors at an elderly neighbor's house. She accompanied the wheel-chair redon neighbor to doctor's appointments, ensured she had hot meals and changed her soiled under garments. She wasn't paid much but it was enough to help put food on the table, clothes on our backs. I never liked seeing her scrub that woman's floors but Mom had to do what she had to do.

I could always count on Mom attending all my school functions. She was at every band concert and every athletic event. And despite my dislike she attended every PTA meeting. I use to tell her that she didn't have to go to the school but she went anyway. Mom made sure all us kids knew not to act up in school because she was going to be there to set us straight.

I remember the day we loss the house I pretty much grew up in. Because my father failed to pay the taxes on the house the city of Baltimore took it forcing us to move to an apartment.

Mom and I were pretty much inseparable. Except for when I was in school, I was seen with Mom. Every Saturday we went shopping, mostly for food. But Mom ensured that there was enough money for us to have a few bites to eat from a vendor at Lexington Market. We use to buy clothes at the old Hecht Company and frequent Woolworth's five and dime. Even once I married and moved out we stuck to our weekend shopping adventures.

Because I worked for many years Mom would attend her Doctor's appointments by herself, but once I earned enough leave, I began taking her. Most of her appointments were no big deal. Her weight was always good, her blood work was normally good, but she did suffer from high blood pressure. That was ok, the Doctors were controlling it. But one day the Doctor said something totally Greek to me, "She has Dementia". At the time I had no idea what Dementia was so I just listened. See, she doesn't know today's date or the day of the week he demonstrated. Still that meant nothing to me, I shoved it off.

I didn't want to believe Mom had some terrible disease. I had no idea of what Dementia was and I refused to find out. In my eyes Mom was still Mom, strong and on top of things.

She was my life and I wanted my life to continue as it was.

Mom didn't say anything about the diagnosis on the way home, she was just Mom. As I think about it now, she was a little more quiet than normal, but at the time I figured it was nothing to worry about. Normally Mom would talk so much I had a hard time getting her to stop. She would complain about everything yet she would laugh and enjoy life. She loved music and would stop complaining about the world when "her" songs played on the radio.

I didn't mention the doctor's diagnosis to my brothers because I didn't believe he knew what he was talking about. As a matter of fact, I didn't say anything for over a year. Because of her High Blood Pressure Mom had regular 3-month appointments so during that year she went at least three times with no mention of the disease.

In my eyes Mom was fine. But I hadn't paid attention to the sudden changes happening right before my eyes. Mom and I spent every weekend together as normal. She would always be ready to go, waiting impatiently for me to pick her up. But as the months of that year passed, she was slower and slower getting ready. There were times when I had to help her get dressed just to get things moving.

The day I realized Mom's doctor was right, devastated me. Though I didn't know a lot about the disease I knew enough to know that it was life altering. I went home, went to my room and cried in silence. I couldn't let my family see that I was weak and wasn't as strong as I tried to make myself out to be.

I hardly cried in life. I didn't cry when my Grandmother, Grandfather or father passed. I didn't cry when we lost our home and I didn't cry when I learned my brother had died of HIV related complications, at least not that people saw. I was a crier in silence and never wanted people to know that I was human.

Even after researching the disease I still didn't want to believe that my Mom was a victim of Dementia's great hold. Until one day my brother informed me that she had walked out the house covered in a mere towel. When he noticed her outside half-dressed, he went outside to bring her in but she fought. According to him it took at least a half an hour for her to return to the house.

It was at the moment he informed me of what had happened that I had to wake up from looking through Rose colored glasses and actually tell him about the disease. It was difficult parting my lips to say "Mom has Dementia, it made her do that." My brother was silent and hurt. He was upset that I didn't trust him enough to tell him about his own mother. I felt bad, like I let him and Mom down.

My brother took Mom's diagnosis like a champ. He excepted it and took on the challenge of Care Giver. I never thought that he being the youngest he would react in just the opposite direction as myself.

The next few years were anything but a picnic. We saw Mom go from a stubborn strong woman, who called me at least five times a week to complain about everything, to somebody who barely remembered the names of her own kids. To prevent her from wandering off, my husband installed a fence around the property in which she lived. We disconnected the gas stove to prevent her from turning it on, possibly filling the house with gas or burning down the house from leaving a pot on.

I also took on the role as Care Giver. It was hard being a mother of two, working full-time and ensuring Mom's needs were addressed, but I knew that if the shoes were on the other foot Mom would not have hesitated. I came over daily to wash Mom, make her lunch or a snack and just talk to her. I believed that talking would help keep her mind fresher longer. We had some really good conversations. We talked about everything from t.v. shows to family to music. But as time marched on the conversations got shorter but I still enjoyed them.

There were days when I would leave Mom's house and drive home in tears. The toll of seeing her transform was getting to me but I didn't want anyone to know. There were times when I would pull into the parking lot of a park to just sit and think about her but mainly to decompress. I just needed to put my Rose-colored glasses on before going home to my family. But most of all, I wanted to forget.

I kept up that facade since her diagnosis and I refused to stop. I didn't want people to think that I was weak, that I wasn't as strong as my youngest brother. I wanted people to think I was strong and capable of handling any situation, just like Mom. But there were times I wanted to walk away from the daily care of her. As a matter of fact, on several occasions I called my brother and made an excuse for not showing up that day.

Every time I cried or had negative thoughts about caring for the person I loved the most I felt like a failure. I felt less like a person and more like a brick wall, cold. I hated feeling like that. I just knew that I was an ungrateful daughter who didn't appreciate anything my mother had done for me. In my mind I knew she would be very disappointed in me and nobody could tell me anything other than that.

I began questioning whether I really loved her. I mean a person who loves somebody will not feel the way I felt. A person who loves somebody would want to spend every minute of every day with that person no matter what. Mentally I felt like I had checked out. That was until one day I received a call from my brother telling me that Mom had been taken to the hospital.

I immediately dropped whatever I was doing, got in

my car and headed to the hospital. My heart had never beat so fast. By the time I got there my brothers were in the waiting room just down the hall from the Emergency Room. They were all gathered in a small group discussing Mom. I asked them how's Mom? They couldn't tell me because they didn't know. We waited for hours and true to form I kept up that strong façade. Unlike my brothers I didn't cry not one tear. I just held my head up high and waited patiently.

Finally, a nurse appears. The nurse directed us to the room in which Mom had been treated. The Nurse gave us no indications as to Mom's condition. I was calm as I walked to her room but just before entering my heart rate tripled, my legs were numb, the rest of my body shaking in fear.

When I turned the corner to enter her room, I saw that beautiful mother of mine sitting straight up on the side of the bed with the largest smile I had ever seen. My brothers smiled back and were happy as a lark. Me on the other hand broke down in tears. I must have cried for over fifteen minutes. I just couldn't close the flood gates. I completely broke down.

My brothers had never seen me cry. They didn't judge me or make me feel weak, they hugged me. They told me that everything was going to be ok. They supported my actions. And when Mom told me that it was ok to cry, I felt so much better. It was shocking that a woman whose awareness was diminishing at a steady pace understood what I was going through.

Today I sit here reading a book to my Mom while she lay quietly in a Nursing home. She barely speaks now, but I can tell she knows who I am. I miss the old Mom, but I feel fortunate enough to still have her. Maybe we don't go to the mall anymore but we still spend every weekend together, just now at her Nursing home bed.

I know this disease will eventually take her but what can I do but love her. As a child, I knew I was a challenge to raise but Mom hung in there and did a good job. As a woman fighting Dementia Mom has been a challenge to care for but I think I'm doing a good job.

The Lady Behind the Curtains

By

Floretta Sharples

Jacqueline Sharples Camper

You all... hurry up and come on! I need to get home before everybody gets there! Mama yelled. Okay Mama we're almost ready, we replied. The story of our life growing up with our "Spiritual mom" who believed in her three girls with all her heart and soul. Our mother was born and raised in a small town that was about twenty minutes from where we lived. And on a weekly basis all of our mother's sisters and brothers along with their children would all get together and spend the weekend in the house that they grew up in, which was always referred to as "up home". Sunday's were super spiritual, and the family had to have breakfast together and attend church together.

Well this Sunday was Easter and boy ole boy did we have a lot to do. Mama would make sure that we had some pretty dresses for this special day! So of course, we had to have some nice little short sets and some pretty-matching bows for our freshly new hair styles. I packed you girls some extra clothes, just in case you mess up your clothes, mama replied. And I have already put the food and other bags in the car. Let's go! OJ! We are leaving, we'll be back on Tuesday. OJ was our father and our mother's husband. He would never go with us, as he would attend the church that he grew up attending as a young boy. And we were all okay with this arrangement in our family.

Praying and driving and driving and praying was something that mama did so very often. Well, come to think about it, she prayed every chance she got! "Praise God! God is good!" were her words of strength and courage.

Oh! We also had a dog and a cat that were just like our brother and sister, so they too would jump in the car and go with us "up home". The dog was the girl and our older sister named her Snooker and the cat was a boy and we all named him Bubba. Up home bound here we go, on this Easter Sunday, our mother praying as we pull out of the driveway. Well girls, shouted mama, God is going to bless you all so much and today is going to be a good day! We all smiled because we loved and believed everything our mother told us. And this belief would become our life, as it is a part of us to this day.

After about twenty minutes or so, we arrive Up Home as my mother prayed, we were the first to get there. Now my mother's father and oldest sister lived in the house, along with our cousin. My mother's mother had died years before the two of us were born.

We walk into the house and we say our proper hellos and off we would go to make sure that everything was ready in the house. My mother seemed to always be the person in charge of everything, except the cooking. Mama did not like to cook, especially for large crowds. But...for her girls, mama would cook for us every single day. And with love in our hearts, we would eat anything our mother cooked for us, even though with truth and love, we all knew that she was not the best cook.

After mama would make sure that everything was fit and all was going well in the house, she would spend some time with her father, who we called Papa. She would sit on the floor next to the chair that Papa was sitting in and they would talk and talk and talk. In those moments, as my sister's and I would get a glimpse of them, they seemed to be some of the most happiest times of my mother's life. She was a daddy's girl! And we were mama's girls! Funny, since my mother was a tough little lady! Crying was not her thing! Love for the Lord and strength was who she was! And to pivot, we were all crybabies! My mother had three little girls that would cry at the drop of a hat! And that part of us she hated ... but would still give us the love and time that we needed to get passed our pain.

Well, after about two hours or so all the family members are in the house "up home" and it is only about 8am in the morning. Sunday morning! Easter Sunday! So, you see...our mother started out really early. She would often say "The early bird catches the worm" ...so get up and be the first one wherever you have to be.

The breakfast is almost ready. My mother's older sister and my cousin would be the one's to prepare the breakfast and my mother would be the one behind the curtains making sure that there was enough food for everybody and that all of the family members were there in the den and ready for Papa. Being Ready for Papa! Being Ready for Papa! And again, Being... Ready... for Papa!

We could not eat, or even began to have conversation until our Papa prayed! And we all, including Papa had to be on our knees before he even began to pray! Oh, and guess what...yes! Mama was the one who made sure that all of us were on our knees and ready to receive this prayer from Papa. And let me tell you...Papa was a praying man who prayed for at least fifteen minutes...and counting!

Papa is still praying... and one of our aunts is starting to get super silly, and you know as small children our patience is sort of short. We start to giggle, and it seemed like the more we giggled the longer Papa prayed! As we silenced our laughter, the prayer eventually came to an end and we would hug each other and eat our breakfast.

After breakfast, we had just a little bit of time to catch up with some of the family members before getting ready for church. Family time was very interesting, my mother would make sure that she spent a little bit of time with all the family members. They would tell her their secrets and would ask her to pray for them. She had to move swiftly as she needed to reach about twelve to fifteen family members. She was super quick and did not miss a beat of what she had to pray about for her beloved family. Of course, our older sister had to get us ready for church because our mother was busy doing the Lord's work, as she would refer to it. We are now Easter Sunday ready! Our older sister has gotten us dressed and we are ready to go! My mother looks at all of us to make sure we are dressed to impress. She was very meticulous about how we looked before going out in the public. The church is crowded, and we are sitting in the pew next to our mother listening to the choir. They are sounding a bit off key, but we are just enjoy sitting next to our mother. She makes listening to them exciting because of her expression. Her love for the Lord resonates as we feel his Spirit moving through us! The preacher begins to preach, and we listen all so diligently and when the sermon is over, and it is time to go back "up home"; it's almost supper time and again it is time for Papa to pray, and praying is what Papa did best. On our knees we all would go, and silence filled the room as Papa prayed and prayed and prayed! We all would take a slight glance at each other and our mother, who was so into the prayer she didn't notice us looking at her. She was keeping it as we say today "100". She was so angelic like as she would sway back and forth as if she was sitting next to God Himself.

We ate our supper and we were a family of tradition. Every Sunday, every single Sunday, we would have steak with gravy and rice. And just because it was Easter Sunday, our tradition would dare not be broken. We are not exactly sure why we would eat this dish every Sunday and we never really asked because it was more about family time. Our family and the bond that we had was stronger than a mere, why do we eat steak and rice with gravy on Sundays! Plus, it was really good! My mothers' older sister and cousin could 'burn in the kitchen" in other words they were very good at cooking and baking. Desserts were plentiful! We would have chocolate cake, pound cake, coconut cake and on and on.

After supper, my sisters and I would mingle and play games with our cousins that were close in age. My mother and her sisters would sit on the "screened in porch" and just talk and reminisce about the days of old. My mother's brothers would head back home to spend time with their wives. But for my mother's sisters, it was time to talk and just have what they would say "a good ole time". And it's funny because my sisters and I to this day get together and we find ourselves saying "boy! We are having a good ole time".

We have been running around the yard and playing all sorts of games, some are well known and others, we made up; "Red Light Green Light", "Mother May I", and "Aint No Bears Out tonight Grandpa Shot them all Last Night". I believe we made up the last game.

Our mother and her sisters are still talking and laughing and just loving their fellowship. We as small children would often sneak near the screened in porch to hear them talk. And to no surprise, my mother would be the one that was the most energized! She was always giving her sisters advice and telling them, to do better. And in her stern and raspy voice we heard her say to one of her siblings; "Sister...you got to do better...you are just too mean! God will not bless you honey! You snapping at people on your job. Oh yes! I heard about you and you need to stop it!" My aunt just looked at mama and said you are right. Please pray for me! And just like that they moved on to another subject. Mama was very direct and her family, friends and the community were all okay with that because they all knew, or shall I say we all knew it was coming from a sincere place! She would pray for us all! Especially her three girls!

Mama would always reference everything back to God and His Loving Grace! She was a second-grade teacher during the school year and a driver's education teacher during the summer months. She was a Super Woman to say the least! Oh! hold on to your hats, Mama had more jobs that will be discussed a little later. Mama's sisters and brothers admired her with every fiber of their body. She was the fifth child of nine siblings. And she would say "the fifth child can see some things". As she was clearly not the oldest sibling, she was indeed considered to be the wisest, the strongest and without a shadow of a doubt the most spiritual one! She was always the one behind the curtain when it came to everyone in the family and everyone she encountered. She was always behind us all to make sure that we did our best, that we gave it our all and that if we fell down, we got back up and we did it proudly and boldly and with praising our God above!

Well, it turned out to be a good day as Mama told us it was going to be! And the night was even better, it was time to "turn in", it was time to go to bed. Our playing time as children had come to a halt for the night and Mama and her sisters had concluded their porch time together. Up Home was a place that had five bedrooms and yet it was a place that could hold so many of our cousins and friends. There must have been over twenty people in the house, all ready to go to bed. During the course of the day into the night, friends of the family would stop by. They would get to talking and time would slip away. They were all welcomed to stay the night, for in my mother and aunt's eyes "Night had no eyes" and they wouldn't have their friends driving home alone in the dark of the night. Settling in for the night or "turning in" was not just finding a bedroom or a space in the bed to sleep. It was well orchestrated.

The Lady Behind the Curtains! Our mother would be the master mind behind who slept where. By now, it should come as no surprise that my sisters and I, without a question or shadow of a doubt would be in the bed with Mama! As a matter of fact, all my mother's sister's children would be in the bed next to their mothers. You see, my mother and her sisters would guard their children with their very being! They were all protectors of their family and particularly their girls.

My sisters and I loved our "Mama time" and our routine would be the same as if we were at our own house. Mama would say in her loud stern voice, yet loving and caring tone! "Come on girls get washed up and let's get on our knees and pray!" Thank God for the day and all that He has given you! She was truly her father's daughter. Praying was also what Mama did best. And when times would get rough and troubles would come our way, Mama never changed course, she was like a train on its track! "Get on your knees and pray" she would say over and over again!

The house is quiet and everyone falls asleep...
Morning light has arrived. Time to get up! Time to get up! Mama would gently touch us as to not frighten us. My older sister would get us ready for the day, as my mother had work to do in the house, Up home. It was time for her to get everything started, well at least manage the process! She would make sure that my aunt, her oldest sister and our cousin had enough food to cook for everybody in the house. And Mama wanted to make

sure that we were, Yes, you got it! The first to get dress. You see there was only one bathroom in the house, so the line to getting ready could get pretty long! The early bird is still catching the worm. We were the first to get in the bathroom.

Everyone is up and after about two hours or so breakfast is almost ready. No eating until Papa prays. On our knees we go and Papa prays! The prayers are still long and after ten to fifteen minutes, we all sit down to eat. We have bacon, grits, eggs, homemade biscuits and on and on. It's a lot of people to feed and everyone is getting only two pieces of bacon. Well back home, mama cooks bacon for her girls, and we get at least four pieces of bacon. So, before we could even say that we wanted more bacon, Mama has already whispered in my aunt's ear to slip us two more pieces. And to my aunt's much respect for my mother, she did just that. Again, my mother would not change her routine for her girls just because we were away from home. Now, please understand, mama was not going to have anyone not getting enough food. If she had to run out to the store and get more food or have her brother to run out, she was going to do just that.

Easter Monday and we have just finished our breakfast. Playing time for the children, but not for our Mother and her sisters. They are busy planning our Big Easter Egg Hunt. The Egg hunt is always across the street to where one of my mother's brothers live. He had the biggest yard and trees where the eggs could be hidden well. Time to egg hunt, "come on babies" our mother would say, "time to get those eggs"! Sure enough, our mother was running around the yard helping all the younger kids find the eggs to keep the fun going! She seems to be having as much fun as the children.

Eastern Monday is coming to an end. We had a great time, as we always do when we go "Up home". Night falls upon the earth and it is time to "turn in". Same routine and same sleeping places. On our knees we go and praying and thanking God for another day and all that He had done for us! Lights out and asleep we go.

We get up bright and early on Tuesday morning and we head back home! We actually see Snooker and Bubba for the first time in a day. They were off having their fun with the other dogs and cats nearby. But one thing was for sure, Mama was taking care of them, making sure that they were being fed and was back in their respective areas before night. We would spend the next ten years or so going "Up home". As time went on my mother's father would pass and she would carry on the tradition of making sure we would always have family prayer before our meals.

"Time waits for no one", Mama would say over and over again. Get up and get it done! The Lady behind the Curtains is how we see our mother. She was always behind our dreams making sure we had everything to accomplish them. She was always behind our pain, making sure we were well taken care of. She was always behind everyone, making sure they did the best that they could do.

Reaching back into our mother's life, she had more jobs than we can count. Yet, we as her children, were given quality time with her and we loved and cherished every single moment. She was a good wife to our father, her husband for 59 ½ years. She was more than a schoolteacher, a driver's education teacher, an adult education teacher, a 4-H club leader, a prayer warrior; she would get in the fields and pick cucumbers, and work in the tobacco fields. She would take care of older people and all these things she did not because she had to and not because she needed the money! She did it for the love of God! She did it for the love of people! She did it because this is who she was.

The Lady behind the Curtains was our mother who had a bond so tight and so strong with us that no dark forces of any places could break that bond! She would attend every sporting event that we played or was in. We were cheerleaders, softball players, in the band, on the drill team, in the 4-H club...we were in a lot to say the very least. And Mama was there for it all, cheering with us, running with us and most of all still praying with us and for us.

As time moved on and Mama was getting older. We knew it was time for her to go and be with the God she served all her Earthly days. We were all older and moved away from our hometown and would often times go and visit with Mama. The bond was still as strong as ever. Yet on one of our last visits, we noticed a difference in Mama.

The things that she would say to us before we would leave and journey back to our homes was not quite the same. She would normally say to us to be careful on the highway, make sure to call and let me know you got there safe, Keep God ahead! I'm praying for you!

Ahhh...Not this time... Mama looked at us and she turned her head and looked out the window and then she said, "God's got you!" And in those moments, we all knew exactly what those words meant. Our mother, the super woman, our hero and yes, our shero! The most prevalent, The Lady Behind the Curtains, had done her job! She was ready to go Home to be with God and reunite with her father and mother and all that had passed before her. Yes! Yes! Mama was Heaven Bound! And as one may think, it was a sad moment and indeed we know we are going to miss her; however, the moment of our final goodbyes was very warm felt. Our mother superseded being a daughter, pray warrior, sister, teacher, wife, mother, friend, and all!

The Lady behind the Curtains, our mother, in Heaven she sits! And on God's right side I know she sits! Our Angel, our mother continues to watch over us with her Heavenly Father and once in a while, we feel her presence and we know that just like a butterfly catching her wings to fly. Our mother helps us to catch our wings so that we can fly above life's storms. And we continue to honor her and dare to walk in her footsteps as she truly was a jewel of a woman!

They Call me Mel

by

R.C. McDonald

They call me Mel, Melanie Mason to be exact. I was born on this tiny little island. An island where passersby waive and say hello; An island rich in history unknown to most. I was raised on this island. As of now my skin is darker than most, yet still lighter than others.

But in the past, I faired lighter than most. Some twenty years ago my hair was adored by most, but today it's shunned by most. My nails were barely visible at one time, now they are seen by many. My money use to take me far, it now barely gets me through the week. My eyes, though resembled others, look differently at the world as the world looks differently at me.

As this island became to know my kind many centuries ago the introductions weren't quite pleasant. Some managed to walk to the shore, heads down, while others floated as unwanted cargo. We unwillingly moved from house to house, town to town, owner to owner. At times we belong to the Spaniards, at times we belonged to the British, at times we were Confederates, ultimately, we became citizens of the United States.

In my early days I enjoyed the riches earned of my family. Compared to most on the island we lived like Queens, Kings and every royalty position in between. The previous generation slaved hard to assure my generation was previewed to the same riches as those lighter than us. We owned a good portion of the southern part of the island as my father acquired several hundred acres as homesteads for descendants of those who walked to shore. We were those to be adored and we were those to be hated.

Our empire, as daddy called it, included the first black own bank, the first black own insurance company and the only crab canning company on the island and ultimately the state. Most blacks loved us for providing jobs, for helping them secure homes, for helping them feed their families while others hated us for those very same reasons. At the time we were pretty much left alone by the whites as they felt we lived on substandard land on the water and we wouldn't have deposited much money into their banks, regardless.

My parents, uncles and aunts worked tirelessly growing the businesses. There were many days I was kept under the watchful eye of my grandparents while my parents worked from sunrise to sunset. At one point I had forgotten what they looked like as they left before I got up for school and returned home after I was put to bed. At times I could hear them talking when they entered from their long days, but I couldn't quite make out what they were saying. As time marched on my mother began returning home early enough to put me to bed, but by that time I was old enough to put myself to bed. When we spoke, she would emphasize over and over again about doing well in school as she needed me to help her father run the businesses. "Mel" She said to me one warm summer night. "You are the oldest. You need to set a good example for your younger brother and sister. You are about to turn twelve. By your fourteenth birthday I expect you to replace me at the cannery." She continued. "But I don't know how to work in a cannery." I replied. "True, so starting next week, you will no longer be attending school. You will accompany me to the cannery." She explained. "But mom." I cried. There is to be no more conversation she emphasized.

Mom meant every word she said. That next Monday she woke me up at 5:00 a.m., fed me, then dragged me to the cannery. I had only been at the small building on the north side of the island maybe two times. It was just down the street from the old paper mill and a couple of miles east of the fort that never saw action. It was small in comparison to the mill but it made money canning crab meat and other sorts of fishy things.

As we walked into the small waiting room I was greeted by my aunt Josephine. "Good morning my little Mel." She said enthusiastically. "Hi Aunti." I replied. "Are you ready to learn the business, you know we expect you to be runnin' this place in a couple years." She asked. "I don't know." I replied. "Josie, she's ready whether she knows it or not." My mother said as she pulled me by my left arm through the door to where the canning was done.

The canning room was pretty large, about as long as two of those buses that carry people around in the big city just south of the island and as wide as the distant from one base to another on a baseball diamond. Resting on the back wall were four long old wooden tables, each holding many tall baskets of live crabs. I broke away for just a second to take a look at the moving crustaceans as Mom walked into a small room. It looked as if they were fighting to claim their territory. They were pretty darn big, blue in color. I felt sorry for them when their beady little eyes turned my way.

"Excuse me little girl." A worker said as he picked up one of the baskets.

"What you goin' to do with that?" I asked.

"Cook them, then open them then get all the meat from their fat big bellies."

"But you will hurt them."

"Well that's what happens when you get caught", The tall dark man said before carrying the basket to a large pot of boiling water. I cried as he poured the crabs into the hot water to seal their faith of certain death. Those crabs didn't do anything to that man and now he's killin' them.

When Mom return, she hands me a white over coat like the one's in the doctor's office, and instructs me to put it on. At first, I resisted, that was until she gave me the look of death. Though Mom worked a lot, she was around enough to ensure we knew who was boss and at this stage it only took a look of her eyes for us to remember. After putting on the coat she walked me to the man who had just ended the lives of those innocent crabs. "Jacob, this is my daughter, Melanie. For the next few weeks you will be training her. Is that clear?" Mom ordered. But she's a kid he said upset. "It's either train my daughter or go home and tell your family that you can't feed them because you lost your job." Jacob looks at Mom then looks at me. "Come on." He then said.

For the next eight hours I followed Jacob around the cannery. There were about fifteen other workers, all of whom at times pointed, looked and giggled at this odd couple. Jacob barely said one word to me but it didn't matter cause I just wanted to leave. I could tell he didn't really care for me but most of all I could tell that he hated my mother. I didn't dislike Jacob at that time, but to me he was just some old man being force to spend time with me. I know I call him old, but in reality, I later found out that he was just barely twenty. "Have a good evening Miss. Melanie." I shockingly heard him say. "I'll see you tomorrow." I replied as he nodded his head then walks away.

Over the next couple of weeks Jacob and I became friends; teacher and student. He explained to me how the cannery operates, the roles of all the people that work there and why they prepare the crabs for canning in the way that they do. He also introduced me to the other employees whom by that time had grown to accept me and I them. They even gave me a nickname, Mel. For some reason Jacob and Mom seem to get along better after she called him over for a talk last week. Within another two weeks I was able to work by myself. Though I missed going to school with my friends I accepted my new job at the cannery.

By the time I turned fourteen Mom had stop coming to the cannery, leaving me and now Manager Jacob to run the place. Mom rarely got out of bed and for some reason didn't eat much. She started turning darker with each passing day. Dad spent much of his waking moments tending to her and not running the other businesses. "Daddy. Is mom ok? She doesn't look like herself." He didn't say anything, he just walked away. So I went into the room daddy setup for Mom on the first floor of our Division St. two-story home. "Mom are you ok?" I asked. She closed her eyes then laid her head back.

"No." She replied. "Your birthday is in three weeks. I'm just hoping I will make it to see you turn fifteen." I looked at her in shock as she closed her eyes again. "Mom, what do you mean?" I screamed. "I'm dy…" "NO!!!" I interrupted. My father burst into the room then looks at me. "Why didn't you tell me." I cried. "We didn't want to worry you." He said. I ran out the room never to see my mother alive again, she passed two hours later.

Mom's funeral was hard on all us kids, we didn't expect this, we didn't want this. The only thing we wanted was our mother. How could our parents keep this from us? They must had known for a while. No wonder they all of a sudden took me out of school and made me learn how to kill crabs. I was pissed.

The crew at the cannery were great after my mother's passing. They worked hard to make sure I didn't have to work hard and that I had time to mourn. "Mel." One of the worker's said as I returned to work some four weeks after the funeral. "We missed you, so sorry about Miss. Sara." The young lady said giving me a long hug. "Thanks Gerdie for all your help with my family. We appreciated all the meals you made for the family and for the repass." I said. "No problem. Your family has been good to me and my family." She stated. "Take your time getting back into things, we've got you covered."

It took more than three months for me to get somewhat close to where things were prior to Mom's death. I still found it difficult to say anything to my father despite his many attempts to be my father again. I loved my father and all but I hate that he robbed me of quality time with my mother. He would forever remember this time as I rebelled, he would forever lose his prized debutant daughter.

Work was my best friend; work was my family. Home became a distant memory as this small area of the island slowly replaced it. Many nights I slept on the beach after working twelve-hour days. I rarely spent a dime; My hair went ungroom; My nails grew uncut; My health went unchecked.

The cannery's business exploded during that time. Business was always good and it always made great profits. But at that time, we were making triple the profits than just one year earlier. The staff and I were excited but it was hard keeping up with the additional orders in such a small building. Well, small compared to what we needed. One day I approached Jacob to ask what he thought of buying the old woodshop next store and expanding the cannery into it.

"Hmm." He said. "I think that's a good idea." He agreed.

"Great, let's go see if we can get it." I said.

That next day Jacob and I approached Mr. Loyld Arthur, owner of the empty old woodshop next store. We proposed a deal to purchase the building. Mr. Arthur didn't want to sell the building so he proposed a deal in which the cannery could lease. The leasing option would require a rental fee of ten percent of the weekly income and two cents per can processed. The terms of the lease would terminate at the end of ten years or when the cannery's weekly income fails to earn Mr. Arthur more than two thousand dollars a week for four weeks. If the contract is terminated due to a lack of income Mr. Arthur had the option to take ownership of the cannery. Confident Jacob and I agreed to the terms and several weeks later production commenced at the old woodshop.

With production at both plants in full swing revenues increased another one hundred percent. Mr. Arthur was making more money than he ever did as the woodshop owner and my bank account could settle the national debt. To thank my employees for all their hard work I issued each of them two-hundred-dollar bonus and ten percent raises. The future looked positive with orders exploding.

Jacob left the cannery one year after marrying his childhood sweetheart and moved across country with his new wife's family. Since his leaving I promoted Gerdie to Assistant manager. I knew she didn't have the experience as Jacob but neither did I when I took the job. I kept her under my wings to give her the best chance of succeeding. She learned fast giving me confidence in her abilities to keep the cannery going as I worked on a project important to me and other blacks on the island.

I'd somewhat gotten over the death of my mother but I still refused to cut my hair and nails. My hair, though coarse, had grown down near my butt. I kept it in a ponytail. Many women envied the softness and length of the thick ponytail and wanted to know my secret for growing such hair. My nails were about six inches in length and would have been longer had I stopped breaking them.

It had become evident that the island was slowly changing for the dismay of the hundreds of blacks living in our section of town. Though blacks were scattered throughout the island the vast majority lived within the borders of the acreage established by my father. The homes built on that acreage are now being threatened by expansion of tourist accommodations along the coastline. You see, the property included over twenty miles of beach front, all dotted with old wooded homes belonging to black residents. I knew I had to take on this mission to save my friends and relatives from losing the homes they worked so hard to own. But I also knew that I needed help. I needed help from the very person I left behind years earlier, my dad.

My dad and I hadn't seen each other in over two years. He's tried to contact me but I didn't want anything to do with him. I wanted to forgive him but I just couldn't, though I thought about him every single day. In the last few weeks, as I worked toward saving our little part of the island, I decided to reach out to him. My father loved the people on this island

and I was confident that he would not let anything happen to the people he has helped in the past.

After turning the cannery over to Gerdie I made my way to the house I grew up in, where my father still lived. Nervous, I put my key in the lock and prayed that it still opened the door, and it did. As the door opened to the living room it brought back so many memories of my prior life. My father walks down the steps to notice me standing. He smiles and begins to cry. The years hadn't taken a toll on him, he looked the same as he had the last time we were together. He walked to me. "My lovely daughter. I missed you so much." He said. "I'm sorry dad, I realized that you and mom were just protecting me. I was bad." I apologized as I began crying. "You've let your hair grow and your nails." I shook my head in agreement. We talked for several hours reminiscing; Strategizing on how to fight the tourism growth.

Our plan was for my father to fight the county on the expansions and I would work with the residents to petition and fight. For months, I sat up a table at the beach closest to the point in which the city planned to take over to meet with residents. We strategized to help fight the acquisition of our homes. Later Mr. Henry Nichols and his family lost their home by some outdated land permit. They said that his house was filed under a plan in place by the Spaniards some two hundred years ago. The family fought the acquisition and lost, forcing his family into the streets. I vowed that would never happen to another one of our people.

As the city attempted their expansion, my organized group of residents gathered on the beach and waited for city officials to arrive. The island's officials had plans of destroying several other homes on technicalities all of which in the area in which our people lived. Here they come I remarked to the group of about sixty residents. "Do you think they will listen?" Mr. Frost, a local store owner asked concerned. "I don't give a dam." I said as four white men got out of the black sedan.

"Wow." One of them said shocked.

"So you nice people are here to greet us?" Another man asked.

"Why are you here?" I asked.

"Oh and just who are you?" The first man asked.

"Mel, they call me Mel."

"Well Mel, as you most likely know we are here to inspect these properties." He answered.

"And for what reason?"

"As you most likely know we are acquiring these properties in the next week."

"But as you may not know is that we are not going to let that happen."

Our organized group formed a line blocking the

men from crossing. Outnumbered they turned around, got in their cars then drove away. The group cheered giving each other hi fives. The residents walked around with a feeling of accomplishments. But I knew this was just the beginning, celebrating was pre-mature.

My father and I met that evening at the house. After informing him of the day's events he slowly walked a few feet in a direction opposite of myself. He stops, turns toward me, head down. "Mel." He said. "We are fighting a losing battle. " He continued. I looked at him in shock. He was never a man to give up, he was a fighter, a warrior. He believed in persevering until you accomplish your goal. He believed in not giving up. I was disappointed. "I spent many hours at the courthouse this week to find that some of that land in which we are fighting to preserve had been given to us on a land lease agreement. The agreement terms were to conclude after twenty years or when either party, that is the city or resident owners, had completed an obligation of twenty years and wish to pull out of it. Mel, it has been well over one hundred years. The city has decided to take back the land. We have no recourse in this matter." Despite his finding I was upset over his lack of concern for the folks who are about to lose their home. As I looked at him, for the first time I noticed his aging face full of graying hairs. "It must be because he's getting older." I thought to myself as I walked to a fireplace several feet away from where he was standing.

Above the fireplace is a long wooden mantle holding many family photos. I carefully looked at each photo trying to figure out our ages. One of the photos caught my eyes, a family photo of myself, sister Clare, brother Anthony, my dad and my mother. I picked it up, eyes clouding, as I stared at my mother. The picture was taken on my twelfth birthday, just one year prior to her death. She looked very happy as all of us kids surrounded and hugged her. You know, it made me feel that I lost six years of happiness with dad because of my stubbornest. He has always been a good man who took care of his family. I felt like crap when I realized that my father had aged and I wasn't there.

Then I realized that he wasn't the only one who had aged, I had too. Here I was now twenty-three years old. I had changed so much. My hair is now almost down to my butt, sort of nappy, and braided in multiple ponytails. My fingernails were so long that I could barely pick up a coin. As I look in the mirror just above the mantle, I see myself and I don't like what I had become. I broke down in tears sparking my dad to run toward me. He was always my protector and I knew he would always be my protector. "Dad, I don't like what I see in the mirror." I said. "What do you mean?" He asked. I turned toward the mirror ensuring my dad stood next to me. We both looked at my reflection. "I feel ugly." I admitted. He stroked my long ponytails then smiled. "You are beautiful." He replied. "And I know you're not giving up on the land issue." He continued. "No I'm not. " I said. "You see, you are beautiful."

During the next few months, I rallied the groups to fight the city's plans of taking over the land. On many occasions I was arrested and spent the night in jail. With each arrest I argued to the judge that the acquisitions were illegal. Though I knew I was singing to a dead choir I kept fighting, as one by one, families were force out of their homes. As the months passed, the number of group members shrunk. The battle was hard and most couldn't handle this horrid fight with the city. But every day I was at the beach waiting for the city to approach the next parcel of land. "Mel", city officials would finally call me. "I see you are here again." They would say to me when they arrived. "Yes I am." I replied in a stubborn voice. Before the day was over city officials would evict another person from their home after my attempt to stop it. They always had a police car accompanying them as they knew I would have to be dragged down to the station.

On March 2 1996, city officials arrived at Mr. Benton's house, and like always I was again there waiting. As with other times I stood in front of the front door waiting for them to serve eviction papers. Officer Johnson, who had been handling the evictions from the beginning walks toward me. "Mel." he said as usual. "I see you are here again." He continued as usual. "Yes I am." I replied as usual. So as I waited for him to threaten to take me to jail he looks at me then hands me a brownish piece of paper. It read that the evictions are to cease at once. It concluded that all but the first ten homes are to be returned to its previous owners per rulings of the island's municipal court. Officer Johnson holds out his right hand. I reached out my left hand, trying to avoid breaking my now twelve-inch nails, to shake his right hand. "Between your father's daily visits to the land commissioner and your screaming we found documentation that the land belonged to these people." Officer Johnson explained. "Mel, take care."

I saw Officer Johnson most every week until he moved off the island. He turned out to be such a wonderful man who was just trying to do his job. I moved back in with my father, until I married some four years later. The residents of the town celebrated their independence at the community hall we call the Rendezvous every March 2. To this day most families still live in their homes but some have sold out to slick talking investors. The faith of our town remains to be seen as that next generation takes over. Today, I still have yet to cut my hair or trim my nails refusing to do so until my time on this Earth is over.

I visit the beach every day, sometimes alone sometimes with my grandchildren. I stay for hours welcoming visitors. They look at me, see the hair I have yet to cut and the nails longer than a yard stick. They ask my name and I tell them, they call me Mel.

The Colors

by

Alise Naomi-Ann McDonald

You with the sad eyes. Don't be discouraged. She sat
looking out as the mountains passed her by swiftly while the
locomotive pushed its way through. They were just as
beautiful now as they had been ten years ago. She was weary
of what was to come. She received a letter in the mail that
forced her away from her seemingly perfect world. She left a
life of happiness just to roll into a past she tried desperately to
forget. She traveled for over eight hours until the train came
to a stop. She looked down at herself and smoothed the
wrinkles in her skirt. She stood up cleared her throat, grabbed
her bag and headed for the exit. It only took a few seconds for

them to adjust as she carefully climbed down the
steps of the train. She looked around and in front of her was a
sign

 – Baltimore. She was back and she was immediately
 scared. It's hard to take coverage in a world full of people –

 She walked off the platform and found a seat. They said
they would meet her inside by the coffee shop. She waited and
waited and waited until two hours had passed. She stood up,
walked out to the taxi stand and got in an awaiting taxi. She
told the driver the address and he took off
 "Visiting?" the driver asked as she looked up.
 "Yes, hopefully for only a couple of days."
 "Baltimore is a great city, so many things to do."
 "Yes I know, I grew up here."
 "Oh nice, I just got here ten years ago."
 "I see."
 She was not in the mood to talk so she stopped.
 They were driving on I-83 headed north until it ended at a
lonely two-lane road, Greenspring Rd.. They take a left then a
few more turns they arrive at her destination. She had the
driver drop her off at the gate to the property. "Thank you."
She said. "You are quite welcome. If you need a ride back to
the station, my name is on this card.", The taxi driver replied
handing her a business card. She took the card then shook her

head in agreement. She grabs her bag from the back seat of the taxi then watched as the driver drives off. She turns to see her destination, where an iron fence separated her from the property.

Attempting to enter, she pushed her shoulder against the gait which immediately opened. On the other side of the street there were large Cherry Trees. Having just finished blooming they were covered with fresh green leaves. It was beautiful here. She loved and hated that place. It was a mile from the gate to the front door. As she had not walked a mile in quite a few years she was tired when she arrived. Eager to enter her destination she rang the doorbell, but no answer. She rang the doorbell a second time and still no answer. Growing impatient she tried the door knob to find the door open. Shocked she walks into a rundown dirty Georgian Mansion, clothes scattered everywhere, dishes were on trays, the smell of alcohol permeated through the air. She tipped toed over the scattered trash when she heard footsteps. A middle-aged woman with flowing brown hair and auburn eyes starts strolling down a staircase leading to the second floor. The woman was wearing a bright red and blue kimono style rob, underwear and a bra. As the woman reaches the bottom step, she sees her. "What are you doing here?" The woman asked as she continues toward the kitchen hitting red solo cuts on the way. The girl follows her.

"You asked me to come." She replies.

"No I didn't, why would I want to?" The woman responds in a harsh voice. The girl's chest started getting heavy. She was getting angry and ready to lay the woman out.

"I wrote it." A voice rang from the living room said. As she turns toward the voice a young boy with bright eyes walks in the kitchen.

"Mitchell, why did you write her?" The woman asked.

"Because she is my sister and she deserves to know what's going on Mom." The young boy approaches the girl and gives her a warm embrace.

"I've missed you Elaine, thanks for coming."

"You're welcome, but you said the letter was from Cheyne."

"Oh so you can't even call me mom anymore?"

Elaine looked at Cheyne and couldn't believe her eyes. It was ten in the morning and she was drinking a glass of whisky.

"When you start acting like my mother then I will call you Mom. Just look at this place it's a mess" Cheyne said as she shrugged her shoulders and looked around. It's hard to take courage in a world full of people. "Mom fired Rebecca." Cheyne rolled her eyes at the boy. Elaine and Mitchell walked into the living room. Cheyne stood at the door.

"How long are you staying?" Cheyne asked rudely.

"Until after the funeral."

"Making sure he is really dead, is that it? Well you got your wish, he is dead."

"Cheyne, I am here cause it has been ten years. I thought we could move on."

"Move on, move on?" Cheyne said irritated, waving her finger.

"You're the reason he is dead." Mitchell said grabbing Elaine's hand.

"You're the reason Mitchell has only seen his father through bars." Elaine stood.

"Did you expect me to standby while he beat you day in and day out. How could I do that. He could have killed you.?" Her cheeks became wet.

"Whatever daughter. He was a good man."

"Mom." Mitchell said as he looked down.

Cheyne stared at Mitchell until he didn't have the courage to say what was on his mind. Cheyne left for her room and didn't come out until the next day. Elaine was in Mitchell's room helping him tie his tie for the funeral. "I wonder." Mitchell said slowly. "I wonder if I can come live with you?" Elaine looked shocked into his eyes where she saw pain. It was the same pain she felt as a child. She remembered cleaning her mother's blood off the steps or getting her up to her room and cleaning the wounds. No child should have to deal with this. "I don't know if she will let me, but I'll try."

-You can loose sight of it all. The darkness inside you can make you feel so small.-

The funeral ended. There wasn't a large crowd, but a good number. At the end Elaine went up to the minister.

"I am sorry for your loss." The minister said sadly. She didn't really feel the same way. She mourned her father the day he hit his mother.

"Thank you, I wonder if I could ask for your help."

"Yes, of course."

"It's for Cheyne, um I mean my mother."

"Yes continue."

"Well, she is an alcoholic. Well, look, all I want is for Mitchell to be safe."

"Oh, I see. You know there are many programs for alcoholics. But she has to be willing to put in the work."

"Do you think you can present them to her tomorrow. I can make lunch."

"Yes I would be happy to."

-Show me a smile then. Don't be unhappy. Can't remember when I last saw you laughing. –

"Cheyne the minister is here. I've made lunch." Elaine said. She spent the entire night cleaning the house. She couldn't have Minister Brown coming into a pig sty. Cheyne fumbled down the steps.

"Hello Minister, we are fine it you are checking up on

us." Cheyne said clearly drunk as her words were fumbled.

"I'm glad to hear it." He rubbed his nose smelling alcohol as Cheyne approached.

Elaine was a little nervous about the visit so she sent Mitchell to a friend's house, fearing the Minister would get ugly.

"So Elaine, what did you make me for lunch?" Cheyne's attention went to Elaine.

"Turkey sandwiches, potato salad and chips."

"Sounds good, I'm definitely hungry."

Elaine, Minister Brown and Cheyne took seats at the dining room table and they all began serving themselves.

"So Cheyne, I understand that this has been very difficult for you. I was just wondering if you might want to join our grief group at the church?"

"Grief and why would I need that."

"Cheyne." Elaine said softly.

"I think it would help especially with your drinking." Elaine continued.

"What's wrong with my drinking?" Cheyne snaped.

"All you do is drink. As a matter of fact your drunk right now. The drinking has got to stop." Elaine insisted.

"Don't you dare tell me what I can and cannot do."

"Cheyne, we just want the best for you and Mitchell." Minister Brown explains.

"No, it you wanted the best for me, you would leave me the hell alone." Cheyne yelled.

"And you, you." She said pointing to Elaine.

"Are no longer welcomed in this house." She continued.

"Well if I go, so does Mitchell. I will take him with me."

"You fuckin bitch." Cheyne angrily said as she pushes her chair behind her and leans across the table. She then smacks Elaine clear across the face.

"Cheyne!" Minister Brown yells as Elaine grabs her face.

-    This world makes you crazy and you've taken all you can. –

"I have had enough of this." Elaine yells as she sobbed.

"You have blamed me for everything. Blamed me because dad loved me more. Even though I hated him because I love you. I never wanted to see you hurt. I tried to help you over and over again but to no avail. You are sick and you need help. If you don't go voluntarily, I will get a court order." A sob burst out as the Minister tries to comfort Elaine. "It's always been about you, always. If you want Mitchell so bad take him." Cheyne insist as she starts to leave the room. "All Mitchell and I ever wanted is our mother."

Cheyne turned to look at her daughter and for

the first time she saw how grown up she was. She was an adult. She turned back around and went into the kitchen and started to grab a bottle of whisky. She felt the curve of the handle and the coolness of the glass. She left the bottle in the kitchen and walked out the back door.

- Just call me up cause I will always be there. –

It was late at night, Elaine had tucked Mitchell into bed, waiting for her mother to return. It was midnight and no Cheyne. Elaine put on a sweater and her flip flops and left the house. She walked down the patio, she saw nothing. She even walked pass the barn and still no Cheyne. Elaine walked until she got to the big willow tree. There was a bench underneath the tall tree. Even though it was pitch dark Elaine was able to make out the figure of her mother sitting still on the bench. Relieved to find her alive and as well as could be Elaine walks and leans against the rough bark of the tree. Nothing was said for a while. The sounds of singing frogs and hundreds of crickets were the only sounds to be heard.

As Elaine waits for the right moment to speak to her mother, she notices several shooting stars. She was hoping that was a sign that everything would be ok. Her hopes seem to come true when Elaine notices Cheyne closing her eyes and seemingly making a wish. Cheyne then turns and said "You're right." Elaine said nothing, she just listened. "I'm not a good mother and maybe I drink too much." Elaine, shocked, looks in Cheyne's direction. "Alright, maybe a lot." Cheyne shrugged.

"Will you go to rehab?" Elaine asked. She waited for several minutes while Cheyne thought. When Cheyne finally spoke, her words were clouded with tears, she was crying for the first time in Elaine's memory. "Yes, yes I will." Excited, yet cautious, Elaine sat on the bench next to her mother and grabbed her hand.

"I should have never hit you, I'm so sorry." Cheyne apologized. Elaine was moved at her mother's admission, so much so that she laid her head on her mother's shoulder.

A week had gone by and Cheyne and Mitchell were packed and ready. Cheyne was going to a treatment center that would keep her for at least six months. Mitchell was moving with Elaine. "You be good boy. I love you I'll be back before you know it." Cheyne said before turning and walking to Elaine. "As Cheyne approaches Elaine she smiles, looking lovingly in her eyes. "I don't know how, but you turned out to be an amazing young woman." She said. "Yes, the odds were definitely against me." They laughed. "I'm proud of you mom." Cheyne smile, hearing her daughter call her mom for the first time in years brought tears to her tiny brown eyes. "No matter what trouble you get yourself into I'll be there for you. I'm just sorry it took a letter and a ten-year-old to bring our lives together."

–And I see your true colors shining through.---

Rose's story

by
R.C. McDonald

By the time I turned fifteen I had two kids. By the time I turned 25 I had been blessed with another six bundles of joy. It wasn't that I liked kids, it was that I was stupid, over and over again. I liked my kids and all but I liked sex better. On many occasions I thought that if I reversed that I wouldn't have so many kids. But me being me it took many years for me to take my own advice.

Most of my kids were pretty darn good, but then there were the other six. I swear those four girls and two boys drove me to drink. Ok, it's not that I didn't drink before them but that's not here or there.

Growing up in the small town of Louisburg, North Carolina in the early 1950's there wasn't much for them to do.

When not at school they spent most of their time fighting each other, fighting the neighbor kids and attempting to fight me, but they knew better.

I remember my oldest son Ned came home from school one day with the nastiest big attitude. Thinking I was some little prissy nobody he came in yelling at me, telling me that I better not ever tell him what to do because he is the boss and that was it. He threw his notebook violently on the floor then stumped into the room he and his brothers shared. Man I looked at him with my blood boiling hot enough to heat the core of the Earth. Then I took my hundred-pound body into that room where he was standing, taking off the shirt I worked a lot of hard hours to buy.

Give me that dam shirt I told him as he throws it on his brother's head. That arrogant boy had the nerve to just stand there staring me down so I stared back at his little black ass. He took a step toward me and I took two steps toward him.

"OOOOh Ned's in trouble." Stan, the youngest said removing the shirt from his head.

Ned looks at Stan then looks back at me. I kept walking toward Ned, my right-hand balling. I was hot. Ned felt the Devil in me and started walking backward.

"Ned you're gonna die to day." Stan said laughing.

"I'm sorry Mama, Mama I'm sorry." Ned cried falling to his knees.

I didn't need to say a word. Ned knew by the look on

my face that he better had gotten himself together or it was gonna be his last day on this tiny little Earth. Yeah, I saw the fear in his face and yeah, he was scared but I didn't give a dam. I wanit Ned to remember this day for the rest of his life. So, I took another step toward him, then another until I was right in front of him without blinkin' an eye.

"God, help me!" Ned screamed blocking his head with his arms.

"I don't wanna die. I swear I don't wanna die." He cried louder.

I could tell Ned thought that all that cryin was gonna get him out of his situation, but nah. Slowly, I sat my body in front of his 5 ft. 10-inch cryin' self and it didn't even matter that he was a whole foot taller than me. I sat there with my legs crossed pulled his head down by the chin then began tapping on his long bumpy nose as the rest of his body joined his nose. My angry eyes glared into his watery eyes as the taps got harder, longer and more irritating. My boy pleaded with me to stop but I refused. As a matter of fact, the more he pleaded the harder the taps got. Normally, I would have stopped after a few minutes or so but that boy needed a more powerful dose, so we sat there for over an hour. By the time I was done with him, you would have thought I had beaten him with a leather belt. All my kids were familiar with Rose's tapping torture, I made sure that by the time they were three they were all sensitized to it. Whenever I needed to pull it out I knew they would cry like a hog goin' into the slaughter house.

Once my third daughter, or was it my fourth daughter, hum, I don't remember, after all I'm 89 now, so life has started to run together. Anyway, that girl, Rosary, had the nerve to try and challenge me on Rose's tapping torture. I couldn't believe her, but of course she was named after me.

One day when she was about ten she hit her baby sister Lucy on her tiny brown head. I saw that girl take her left hand and slap it across Lucy's face. That child must have had the Devil in her that day. Then she had the nerve to look at me like she didn't do a dam thing wrong. I shook my head in disbelieve. I waited for my little Devil child to do something to make right. Well she did do something, she walked out the front door and sat boldly on the top step of the house.

I told my other daughter Sarah to look after her baby sister while I took care of her older sister. I didn't believe in beatings but I was tempted to take Rosary and beat that Devil out of that child. But when I saw her sitting on the step I stopped and took three deep breaths. Those deep breaths somewhat calmed me down so I took three more all while she sat ignoring me. Here I am thinking to myself, how in the Hell did I let the Devil take over my child's body, I didn't even remember him asking if he could come in the front door.

But I knew I had to get that child away from that Devil. I sat next to my lovely daughter and began Rose's Torture. We sat there for 2 hours and that devil stayed in my baby. But I was determined to get him out so I pulled both of her long Ponytails from the back of her head and marched her a mile down Main Street to her father's house. Once I told him what she did he took his belt off his pants and let her have it. It took a while but that Devil eventually came flying out of her. She cried so hard and so loud that the Devil couldn't stand it anymore. We then walked home, Rosary quite as a calm summer day. And you know what, that Devil never showed up again because now she knew what was on the other side of Rose's Torture. And even though I would never beat any of my children I knew that a beating was just a mile down the road.

I never married, could never figure out a reason to do so. My kids were ok. They all had the same dad and their dad had always wanted to marry me. Marriage, I thought was for everybody else. I didn't need a man to take care me and my youngins. I made my own money and raised my own kids and I loved not sharing a bed with another human being.

The kid's father, Ned Sr., was a good father. He took the kids many times during the week so I wouldn't go crazy. He made sure they had a good education, that they were well behaved and mostly he made them feel loved. Ned Sr. begged me a hundred times, or was it a hundred and one times to marry him. And every time I said "Please man. That marriage thing ain't for me." And every time he was disappointed. He would lower his head and just walk away.

I always felt bad for Ned but that was the way I felt.

Ned was a good man who never made me feel bad. He treated me and the kids like royalty. He loved me and I loved him, just as we both loved the kids.

As a family, we shared some good times as best we could in the mist of Jim Crow. We would go to the nearby parks and have picnics, we would go to the movie theatre and watch some stupid, yet crazy, people on the screen, mostly white. But that didn't matter we had fun.

Me and Ned celebrated each of our eight children's birthdays by throwing huge parties. We would invite all his family and all my family. Though his family hated me for not marrying Ned, they loved me for being there for him and for being the great mother that I was, if I must say so myself.

Our families loved the kids' birthday parties we threw at Uncle McKoy's farm. There was always plenty of food and drinks and we always played that Jazz. Sometimes the parties were more for the adults than the guest of honor child and that was the way we liked it.

As the kids grew they began to leave the nest. Slowly the house became quiet. It was hard getting use to the quiet so I would play my records all day just for some noise. I really enjoyed my music but I missed my flock more.

Rosary had moved to California with a friend of hers. I didn't want her to go, especially with a man me and Ned barely knew. For what we knew of him he was a Farm Hand's son from a nearby county. To others he seemed like a nice boy but

I always had my suspicions about him. Yeah, his mother and father seemed fine but there was something about him that I didn't like. When she came home and told me that she was leaving to go to California with him I told her that there was no way in hell I would let her go across the country with some stupid farm hand's son. I told her not to go, that I didn't trust him, that she was making a big mistake. Ned on the other had thought it was a good opportunity since there was a lot less Jim Crow out there and lots of jobs. I gave in and she and that man left the next day.

Ned Jr. and my two younger boys graduated school and moved to nearby Raleigh. At first, I worried if they were going to survive living with each other without me supervising. But then I thought, if they really get into it the strongest would survive. And if the strongest survives I'll know who to call when I'm too lazy to carry food from the grocery store to home.

Thank goodness none of the girls followed in my footsteps. They all managed to keep from getting knocked up. To me that was an accomplishment considering their mother's history. That's the one thing I'm so glad they didn't learn from me. Sarah married and stayed childless for many years before giving me my first grandchildren. She was 26 when she was blessed with a set of twin boys. Lucy refused to have kids claiming that I had enough for the two of us.

Ned Sr. had given up on marrying me and had hooked up

with a School teacher from Morrisville. By the time all the kids were gone he had been married ten years. I didn't like the School Teacher but what could I do, it was his life. He should have just waited for me to come to my senses, but I guess waiting fifteen years was a bit long, whatever.

Life alone was going ok. I was lonely at times and wanted some company but it was life as it was. I see some of the kids on a pretty regular basis, except Rosary and my son Lucas. Lucas couldn't seem to keep himself out of trouble. No matter what Ned and I did he always seemed to end up behind bars. At times I wondered if he had some type of mental issue and had considered putting him in an asylum. The only reason I hesitated was because once a person was admitted to an asylum for Negroes there was no way that person would ever live a normal life.

Whenever Lucas was locked up I felt that it was the best for him. I was just waiting for him to end up in a ditch somewhere or swinging from a dam tree. He hated the world. Sometimes I wondered if he was switched at birth because none of my other kids were like him.

Overall life was good. By the time I turned fifty I had saved enough money to retire. I worked as a secretary at the nearby Albion school. I loved working there. The folks I worked with were crazier than I was and that was saying something. It wasn't a day that went by that somebody wasn't kicked out for jokingly threatening to kill the Principle.

I looked forward to my retirement. I had plans of traveling, maybe goin' to see Rosary in California. I hadn't heard from her in several months which was odd cause she used to mail me every two weeks. I worried, I worried, I worried. Somethin' was tellin' me to go look for my baby, but Ned and the other kids told me that I'm just a worry wart.

I ignored them so on the day I retired I caught the southern railroad to Los Angeles. I took the address on the last letter from Rosary and spent three hours finding it. It was some old shack not fit for man nor beast. I almost threw up when I saw that dirty dump in a hole.

I was pissed when I thought about Rosary living in that mess. I wanted to ring the neck of that fool that brought my baby out to this ex-con filled neighborhood.

"Hey lady what you doin' on my walk way." A man walking up the street yelled.

"Lookin' for my daughter." I yelled back.

"Ain't no female here lady."

"Ah, yea there is. Roasary Suthers lives here."

"Oh, that the lady who was here before I got here."

"So she moved?" I asked uncertain.

"You could say that. She dead. The man she was livin' wif killed her."

My heart dropped. For the first time in my life I was speechless. I didn't believe him, I didn't want to believe him. I just knew he had the wrong person, I mean just lookin at him I could tell he wasn't the brightest bub on the strip.

I took a picture of Roseary from my purse and handed it to him.

"Yeah, yeah, that the girl. She dead. They took her to the morgue."

Pissed, I snatched the picture from that idiot's hand then found my way to the morgue. The place smelled like death and in my head it looked like death. It was dark and cold but the people who worked there acted like they were at some type of freekin party.

I walked in that place with authority and walked out defeated. Thank goodness Rosary was not in that place but unfortunately, she had been a visitor some two months ago. They said she was beaten to death so badly that her face had been disfigured. I was shown a picture of her face it was barely recognizable as my baby except the mole on her left chin. The mole had been apparent since birth. There was no doubt that she was gone.

I had to leave her in California cause I couldn't afford to have her taken up from the ground and sent back home. I hoped that one day I could save enough money to have her moved near me, but that was highly unlikely.

That next day I boarded the train home silently cryin' the entire three days back to Louisburg. I worried about Ned Sr.'s reaction to the news about his oldest girl. Ned would tell me that Rosary was his favorite of all the kids. I hushed him every time he said that but I knew he was telling the truth.

I arrived home to a cloudy windy chilly day, too cold for May. Every now and then a drop of rain would fall and the clouds would go from white to very dark. But the weather didn't stop me from heading two miles out my way to Ned's house, he just had to know about Rosary.

Ned opened the door when I got there. He was surprised to see me. He could tell somethin' was wrong, after all we had known each other for over forty years. I didn't hesitate to tell him the news. He took it hard, falling on the floor. I had hoped he would hug me but he didn't. I missed his hugs and I really needed one that day. Instead his wife runs to his side and he hugs her before closin' the door.

A large part of me died with Rosary. I wanted to go back to California and clime in the ground with my baby. I hated that son-of-a-bitch for killin' her and swore I would kill him if I ever saw him.

Everyday for the next two months me and the kids called the Los Angeles Police to see if they caught the guy. And everyday we got the same answer, No we will let you know when we do.

Ned Sr. never came by to see how I was doin. I guess he was too busy with the wife and his other two kids they had together. To me he was a liar. He lied about lovin' me and he lied about lovin' the kids.

Ned Jr. was frustrated with the Los Angeles Police

Department so he decided to take matters in his own hands. He knew the killer was from nearby, so he staked out the house his mama and pop lived in. Ned Jr. stayed day and night rarely goin' home scared he would miss the killer.

One pretty day in October Ned Jr. spotted the killer at the house he had been watchin' for the past four months. He jumped on him from the back and beat him dead. But the deaths didn't stop there, Ned Jr. was killed by the killer's pop before Ned had released the guy's dead body.

We buried Ned Jr. next to a make shift grave we made for Rosary. It seemed fitting that my two oldest babies be buried next to each other. I hoped no more of my babies would lay in the row of graves at the Negro cemetery before I took my place.

By Spring of 1941 Ned Jr.'s wife gave birth to a nine-pound baby boy, Ned III. She was young, only about fifteen and had very little family to help so they moved in with me. Ida was a sweet girl. She respected me and loved her son. But I could tell that motherhood was hard for Ida. There were many times she shook the baby tryin' to stop him from cryin'. I helped as much as I could but I couldn't be there all day cause I had to return to work to help support the three of us.

One day after working a long fourteen-hour shift, I returned home to find the baby and no Ida. I looked all over but she was nowhere to be found. I never saw her again. As Junious, that's what I called him, grew, we became best buddies. I must say, I rather enjoyed raising that little boy.

On Junious' fifth birthday Ned Sr. had the nerve to come knocking on my door. I hadn't seen him in years. He wasn't there for me when Roseary died and kept his distance when Ned Jr. was killed. He had never seen Junious or any of the other three new grandchildren. He looked a little frail like that wife of his was not feeding him, oh well, not my problem.

"What you doin' here?" I asked shocked.

"I came to check on you."

"Oh?" I responded.

"You haven't cared about me and the kids for over ten years." I continued.

Ned Sr. tried to get me to feel sorry for him with a bunch of bull shit excuses. He claimed that his wife was sick and that he had been taking care of her for the last few years. He tried to apologize for not being there when Ned Jr. and Roseary were killed. I didn't bye it for a minute. You could not tell me that in six years he could not get his ass down here. Pissed, I gave him the middle finger then slammed the door in his face. That was the last time I saw him though he tried many times to get the kids to talk me into seeing him. He should have known better.

Life was interesting, I must say myself. I couldn't have asked for a better one. There were ups and downs but thank goodness the ups outweighed the downs. I've missed my two babies over the years but guess what, I'm on my way to join then now. My life did flash before my eyes as I made my way to join them. It was nice and I will miss all the friends and family I'm leaving behind, but I'm ready for the next chapter.

Through The Eyes Of

by
Kendra Grace

The alarm went off at 7:45 a.m., fifteen minutes before work starts. She woke up, rolled out of bed, ran to the bathroom and did all that needed to be done before heading to the Livingroom to log onto her computer. You see, COVID-19 and the stay-at-home order took away her forty-five-minute commute to work, so that was all the time she needed to prepare. If she could figure out how to get everything done in five minutes she would wait until then to wake up and get ready. A morning person she is not, especially since her sleep is broken almost every night due to her illness. Charise sat at her desk, then opened her laptop. As soon as the screen brightened she saw a reminder, "HAPPY BIRTHDAY TO ME!!"

Since the COVID-19 pandemic had everything closed, all plans for celebrating on hold, she completely forgot it was her 41st birthday. With her eyes closed she smiled, raised her hands towards heaven and quietly said, "THANK YOU FATHER for another year of life." After a moment or two she quickly closed her laptop and jumped in excitement. "I'm off! Alexa play "You've been so faithful", she exclaimed.

As she danced, singing to God ...and being thankful for simply still being here, she heard her phone going off in the distance. It's quite unusual for her not to have her phone close by, it is her lifeline. She went back to the bedroom to grab it. Wow, she thought. Twenty-five missed Facebook messages, six missed calls and a dozen missed text messages, and her phone continued to buzz with more alerts.

The joy she began to feel, her heart felt warm and fuzzy as she was eager to read each message. She wondered who reached out. And yes, she was looking specifically for one call, text or post from a particular fella.

Mr. Gavin King. Oh yes, he had her heart and he'd most definitely impacted her life. He knew her like none other. Their story was one for the books. Full of ups, downs, joys and unfortunate pain. Pain Charise wish never existed, especially the pain she caused. They were in a much better place now, a healthy place. He was definitely a priority in making her day special.

She looked and scrolled through her phone. One by one she read the names. Lake, Bert, Mom, her children. What joy that brought to her heart. It was nearly 8:15 and both children had already wished her a happy birthday. That was a first for them especially being that early. She continued down the list, checked the missed call log then jumped to Facebook and no Gavin. Her heart sank with disappointment. It was odd for him to have not contacted her by now, even on a regular day.

"Maybe something's wrong, maybe he's in a meeting", she thought. "I don't know but I'm calling him." She called, the phone rang...no answer. She tried to video chat him, still no answer. "Ok something must be going on."

In attempts to not let her mind wander and fill in the blanks with negative scenarios, which she was famous for doing, she went to the kitchen to make her birthday breakfast; waffles topped with strawberries and whipped cream, bacon, scrambled eggs with green peppers, onions and spinach and to top it all off her famous anytime Bellini's. Those were always a hit for any gathering or function. People requested it all the time, so much so that she often wondered if she could and should try to market and sell her delicious creation. But like most times self-doubt or others opinions of what she should be doing or what others thought of what she was actually doing played too much of a part in her decision making. She had gotten better with that over the last couple of years, but it still reared its ugly head from time to time.

~It's tragic to see the fruit of insecurity and low self-esteem that grows from the seeds of dysfunction and abuse planted in one's youth. When a person's worth isn't lovingly established during the critical, early childhood years, he or she may find that they've become a broken child, living in a grown body, mimicking an adult life.-

As she sat and enjoyed her breakfast the notifications of birthday wishes steadily grew, continuing to brighten her morning. She was pleasantly surprised at the number of people who were reaching out. She began to respond to each message, one by one. She thought, "This is going to take all day," But it was no biggie. You see each year she made it a point to respond directly to everyone who took the time to send a message whether simple or long. It was as if she was saying, I see you and am acknowledging you. Surely if they took time to spread a moment of love, she'd make time to thank them for doing so. Plus, she had no plans of being anywhere, nope not this birthday! She wasn't taking any chances of going out and potentially contracting the deadly virus. Her immune system was already compromised and she had been diligent in protecting her health, and she wasn't stopping now.

Then it happened. Her video chat ringer went off and she saw his face. Her love, her best friend, her Gavin. She took a second to fix her hair just right so it would lay over her midnight blue silk pajama top, the pajama set he had gotten her for Christmas. It was one of her favorites. She connected the call with a smile that went from ear to ear. The twinkle in her eyes as she gazed at him through the phone instantly made him blush before he could even get a word out. "Happy birthday beautiful, you're looking as lovely as ever," he said with his sexy voice.

Barry White had absolutely nothing on him. It made her melt like butter every time he spoke; well, except for the times they found themselves in an argument. Oh no! During those times that sweet voice that could calm her and make her heart go pitter patter would turn into a grating sound that scraped every nerve in her body. The pain it would cause...literally! That wasn't the case this day and hadn't been for quite some time. She was in her happy place, her safe space with him. It was the one moment she'd been waiting all morning for.

"Babe I called you a couple times. Is everything okay?" she asked.

"Yes love. Got pulled into an unexpected meeting and had to present. You know how these things go sometimes" he explained.

"Yeah I know", she mumbled under her breath. You see Gavin was an executive producer for a major record label,

Revolution Records. Though she understood his position and importance in the industry, she still wanted to know why he was just getting around to calling her, especially since it was her day. He could've at least sent a message she thought. But hey, she wasn't about to start a pointless argument. Nope! She was feeling too fine, so whatever disappointment she felt she simply swept it under the rug and moved on.

"So what's your day looking like?" she inquired. There was only one answer she expected to hear. He was making his way to spend time with her after his work day. Anything less than that would definitely cause a problem, a major one at that.

"Well I have a few meetings with a couple of prospective clients. Then I have to run to a store or two and...."

"Whoah, hold up Mr.", she interjected quickly.

"You do realize that...."

"That today is your birthday and if l want peace, I better have seeing you on my list". He said figuring he'd cut her off and beat her to the punch.

"Precisely! Now what time should I expect you?" She said jokingly with a little chuckle in her voice. But to her this was in no way a joking matter. She was serious. Due to work and a dozen other projects he had going on in life, their face to face time was already limited. All she knew was that he should've had something special planned for her birthday.

"Baby relax, I'll be there before 6.", He assured her. That's all she needed to hear. They spoke a few moments more and

as the conversation continued things began to change;
drastically change.

As Gavin showered her with birthday wishes and words of
affirmation regarding the growth he'd seen in her since they'd
reconnected over the last couple of years, Charise's mental and
emotional state took her to a dark place. Whether it was his
words that took her back, the Bellini kicking in or a
combination of both, her mind began to wonder. She had
become disconnected from the conversation. So much so that
she missed the words of love and encouragement he was
giving. In a somber voice, out of nowhere she cut him off.

"Babe I gotta go."

"Why, what's wrong" He asked.

"My head hurts. I need to lay down" She replied.

"You were just fine, what's really going on?" He asked.
Gavin knew her inside and out. Nothing got past him
regarding any changes in her mood or disposition. Not the
ones she tried to hide and not make a big deal about, or even
the slightest ones that she at times didn't even catch. Years of
studying Charise made him an expert of her, sometimes more
than she was to herself.

"I just need to lay down", she exclaimed.

With a slight tone of frustration and hesitation he simply
said, "Ok. I'll call and check on you in a few hours. Take care.
Call me if you need me or if an emergency arises. Love you
pooh." That was his nickname for her.

"Love you too babe, talk to you soon."

She hung up the phone. It instantly rang back. She thought it was him calling but it wasn't so she ignored it. In a matter of minutes Charise's high of birthday excitement dropped to zero. She walked to the living room window to pull open the blinds only to see that the rain and darkness outside was a direct reflection of what she felt internally.

~Without a transformed mind, you'll keep recycling your experiences and watering seeds that were never meant to grow-

Her joy turned into sorrow. Even with all the notifications and calls still coming in, she kept sinking into the abyss of regret and shame. She looked back on her life and began to cry. All she could see and feel was pain. When in her mental space it got quite ugly and lonely. Although she had plenty of memories of great times with so many through the years, it was clouded by devastation. Memories of rejection and abandonment, "daddy issues", dysfunction and abuse of many sorts...the list went on. Trauma that broke and caused the identity of a little "yellow girl" to be altered by life's issues. Issues that shaped her into a young woman living in an identity crisis. She'd developed habits that on one hand kept her "sane", and on the other kept her bound and wanting to end it all at times. She actually tried twice, BUT GODS GRACE kept her, though often she questioned why.

Her ability to see pass her past had become challenging over the years. Although behaviors and toxic mindsets had changed, she constantly relived situations she wished never took place. There were many unfortunate things that happened to Charise, but what plagued her soul the most were the things she did to herself. She was remorseful of moments and time wasted by bad, even horrible choices made. Choices that not only hurt herself but others as well. Recently, she had several conversations with individuals seeking their forgiveness. Though she had received their forgiveness, the consequences and sting of poor decision making gripped her heart relentlessly.

She knew she couldn't stay in this dark place. She also knew that God had delivered her from the destructive path she once lived on. Getting out of the pit she currently found herself in could only occur by seeking and trusting God, but at this moment he seemed so far away.

With tear-stained eyes and lying on her oversized sofa she whispered the words to a song, "LORD I NEED YOUR HELP. JUST CAN'T MAKE IT WITHOUT YOUR HELP." Nothing changed. More lyrics and scriptures began to ring in her spirit and from her lips.

"Sometimes you have to encourage yourself...I speak life, you're gonna live...you survived the worst of times. God was always on my side. There is therefore now no condemnation for those who are in CHRIST JESUS." One by one each song began to encourage her heart. She prayed, "Father, thank you for Your love, grace and mercy. Thank you for forgiving me and causing others to do the same. Thank you for the things I've learned and for causing me to grow continuously. God, I need You! Please help me to truly forgive myself...." She layed there for some time pouring her heart out to the Father. The only FATHER she'd truly ever known.

~In moments of despair you must know where your help comes from. Otherwise, you'll grow weary.

~ Trust in the Lord with all thine heart and lean not unto thine own understanding. In all thy ways acknowledge Him and He shall direct thy path. Prov 3:5-6

She continued to cry, still feeling a sense of shame and inadequacy. She wondered and asked, as she'd done plenty of times before, "Lord, what was the meaning, the reason for all this? Why so much and for so long?"

Although it was her forty first birthday, she felt as if she'd only been truly living for two years. She continued to reminisce and suddenly she heard a still voice say, "Pick up your phone." She knew the voice. It was God speaking directly to her. She did as she was instructed and was amazed at what she saw. Over two-hundred new notifications. She was in complete shock.

First she noticed a text message from one of her dear students she had known and mentored for about ten years now. Rebecca. She was a beautiful, well-mannered and talented young lady, but also troubled. Life for Rebecca had been challenging for some time. Things seemingly "appeared" to be changing for the better; however, Charise could see the signs written all over. She knew if Rebecca didn't start making better choices, she'd soon find herself on a long, destructive journey ahead.

The two had developed a solid relationship which was needed for Charise to help Rebecca through the various changes' life presented her. It's as if she saw herself in Rebecca, the good, bad and unfortunate. She vowed to never let her go through life alone. She'd be to Rebecca what she wished someone was to her at that age. She opened the text. It read...

"Happy birthday darling. I am twenty now and I wanna say thank you for the past decade and some. Thanks for being more than a advisor I'd see ever so often in school. You're the person that has seen everything. From the happy to dark side of my child to teen years, the things others don't know. You've shared stories of your past to bring understanding and help guide me. For such trust and compassion, and no judgment. I thank you so much! I am very honored to have gotten to grow up with you in my life!" 🖤 🖤

The message continued and as Charise read each word, the heaviness she felt throughout the day began to break. As soon as she finished, another message from a childhood friend appeared.

"Reesie, It's ya birthday sis!!!! I hope you are filled with all the joy, love, and fabulous-ness you always bring to so many everyday. You are and have been a blessing through the years. Your growth is amazing to watch. Keep walking in your power and ministry. Be blessed my sister and Happy Birthday! I Love you!"

With each message she read, the burden lifted. The trajectory of her day had fully shifted and she found herself back in the place of praise and thanksgivings. Truthfully better than before. Joy, true joy overflowed within. Her smile was bigger and brighter. Her heart made whole, her mind renewed.

~One day we'll move pass the hurt, laugh at the reason we cried and forgive those that caused the pain. We'll realize the secret of being free comes from allowing God to break the chains. HIS WILL, HIS WAY...Your Faith! -

~It's a new Season, It's a New day!

It was now midafternoon. She couldn't understand where the time went. She was simply glad to be FREE. As she sat on the sofa, from her peripheral vision she noticed something. It made her get up and walk back to the window. She opened the blinds once again and realized the rain had stopped. Not only that, but a double rainbow traced the skies ahead. What originally drew her attention was the single ray of light that shined through the window, hitting the exact place where she laid. She knew without a doubt that God touched her. She also realized what He was showing her concerning her life. She carefully thought about all that had taken place and understood these truths.

-There was beauty in her brokenness, ministry despite all the mess. His plans and purpose unfolded through her pain. HE kept her through it all!

With hands raised and certainly more tears; not of sadness but of a grateful heart, she knew in that moment that God altered her perception and perspective. He clarified her Purpose. He solidified her identity in Him. She was fully encouraged and determined to never look at her life quite the same. Oh no! She was strengthened and made new. Moving forward she vowed to only look at her life
"Through The Eyes of GRACE".

Her next level of living, of BEING had just begun. It was

time for her story to be heard.   TBC.......

MY YESTERDAY, TODAY, MY TOMORROW
by
Heather Tate

The cool air pushing through that bay window could have rocked me to sleep all day, but I got to get up.... I got to get up. It starts TODAY!!!! As I roll deeper in my fluffy comforter.. "ANNNNNN !!!! get up"! I hear in my head, you promised yourself a new life, a new lifestyle! NOW!!! I kick everything out my way including my bestie Earl. Earl looks at me with such disgust as he licks his shining black coat and pries himself from the tangled pile of bedding on the floor. He looks back at me one last time in a huff as he leaves my bedroom in search of a safer place to sleep, because I obviously had lost my mind.

My Earl, I remember the day Alen brought him home as an eight-week-old kitten. It was right after my second miscarriage, everyone kept telling Alen I needed something to take care of and that's when he brought me Earl. Earl has been something to take care of and most of all something to love. Six weeks after my sweet Earl joined our family I found out I was pregnant with my son Trent. That was seventeen-years ago, my God has time flown by. Oh well, no time for reminiscing let me get my butt up and at em!! Its time to shower and hit these bike trails. I promised myself these extra seventy-five pounds will be gone for good as I embrace my newest project, ME!!!!

As I drag myself to the bathroom I notice the silence, I guess my baby boy is off today and sleeping in. I dare not open his bedroom door and disturb him. After my shower I dry and moisture and brush my mop of hair into a messy bun. This is as good as it's gonna get cause I don't see my hair rescuer, Heather, until later this afternoon. I make my bed.

As I'm dressing in my newest athletic gear Earl jumps in the middle of my bed with such Cattitude..... payback from this morning. (Still Silence).... that boy must have been on that game all night I thought. Trent and his boys... Such good guys! He and his friends since pre-k, are some of the smartest kindest hardworking seventeen-year-olds you ever have the privilege of meeting. (Silence)..... Yeah he's knocked out. I pass his room, door shut as usual, to enter our hallway to the kitchen.

Keurig on. Eggs on. Black coffee boiled, eggs on deck! I grab my IPad off the charging dock. I grab my coffee and eggs. Noticing the nearby clock, I see I'm thirty minutes ahead of schedule. As I sit at the dining room table I scroll through the local news, same old same old. Gas prices up, crime up, local schools failing, local grocery stores closing. Shaking my head. Three shootings in the city overnight. Victims ages: twenty-three, thirty-nine and seventeen Damn! I know what that looks like first hand as an ER nurse I see the wounded and fatalities daily. Shaking my head I vividly remember the look and screams of a mother just told of the death of her sixteen-year-old son killed after a gunshot to the head. Dear God!!!! What would I do if.....???? Never mind those thoughts...

Time to hit the road, time to hit the trails. As I go pass my Trenty's room to get my socks and sneakers I cannot resist the urge to kiss his face before leaving. Shoot I pay the bills in here, I have a right to go in his room!! I open his door.... His bed is made, his game controllers are neat, his room is undisturbed..... Where is my SON!!!!

I run and grab my phone off the nightstand in my room, no missing calls, texts, email!!! WHERE IS MY SON!!!!! Trent never would stay out all night from home! He's not that type of child. Desperately I run to his bathroom, nothing not a trace!!!! I'm shaking!!! Where are you son, Trent where are you. ANN pull it together!!!!!

I call his phone, straight to voicemail!!! I text him all caps CALL ME SON PLEASE!!!! I call again and again, straight to voicemail!!! His friends!!!! With trembling hands I go through my contacts, I pull up Omar, his best friend, his right hand, yes Omar knows where Trent is, second ring

"Hey mama Ann" Omar answered.

"Hi baby, have you talked to Trent he's not home." My voice breaks,

"Not recently mama Ann, he wished my girl a Happy Birthday last night on IG." Omar replied.

"What time Omar?" I asked.

"11:29p"

I arrived home around 12a.m. last night. His light was off I didn't open his door. I didn't want to wake him, I thought he had to be to work early the next day. Trent has been working extra hours at Amazon since the beginning of summer, his supervisor Neil admires his hard work and dependability so whenever Amazon has extra hours Trent is always first in line.....I didn't open his door!!! Why!!!!

"All friends and associates, I need everyone in their circle alerted." I explained coming out of my daze.

"I'm sure he's fine mama Ann." Those are the last words I hear as I hang up with Omar.

I know the world we live in, it's horrible realities, it's ugly truths. Boys and men heck even women who are our color don't always make it back home safe, hell some of us get killed in our homes. God help me!!!!PLEASE!!!! I race to my living room, I pass the fireplace, I stare at the mantle.

"WHERE IS OUR BOY ALEN!!!" The perfectly folded American flag remains silent.. Tears, hot tears, no time for self-pitying. I reach from my iPad to use the t.v. remote to turn on the local news, blah blah blah nothing about those shootings last night, nothing... with trembling hands I google local shootings, too much comes up I click on the first thing I see.....

My phone rings it's Omar, " Yes Omar anything???" I say without hesitation. "Nothing yet Mama Ann , everyone says the same thing they talked or texted with him yesterday, yesterday was the last time we communicated with Trent." Omar explains as tears begin flowing out of control. "Ok Omar please keep me posted." I replied. "Will do, he's fine Mama Ann." Omar tried to assure me.

I want to curse scream and hollar!!!! Back to the internet, Local shootings last night I bypass the thirty-nine-year-old's story, RIP ma'am. Seventeen-year-old involved in police shooting, the next story reads. Dear God! Last night a Seventeen-year-old male was fatally shot in a police involved car chase. Victim was seen driving recklessly heading south on 395. Seventeen-year-old evaded the police for seven miles. The seventeen-year-old came to an abrupt stop. Fleeing the vehicle the seventeen-year-old was seen running. Heading north on 395 he was shot several times in the back as he ran from police. The victim died at the scene. Victim has yet to be identified.

My heart stopped cold. I feel nauseous, I feel faint.... Silence..... too much. My mind is racing a mile a second. Who do I call first??.... I know who I have to call. My clammy hands reach for my phone, I dial...... never in a million years would I thought I had to call..... him.......Him, my oldest, judgmental, ultra conservative brother Austin.

I haven't seen or spoken to him since the funeral. I now need him desperately. He's a city homicide detective and has been for the past eighteen years......the phone picks up on the second ring,

"Ann?"

"Hey Austin."

"WOW, you do remember my name and number.

"I know it's been sometime."

"It's been five years Ann!"

"You tried to take my son from me, Big bro! "

"You couldn't even function, you were in no condition to parent, you just lost your husband Ann!"

"I needed my son! He is the reason I'm still standing today."

I think to myself, it's not my fault you and your wife couldn't conceive!!! I could never say that to him I need him. And I definitely couldn't say Austin I would never call you if I didn't have to!!!!! "Trent hasn't been home all night; I don't know where he is, his friends haven't seen him. There was a shooting..." My voice trailed off.

Austin sucks in air and slowly lets it out (I told her he thinks to himself)," I told you, Ann you should've moved from that neighborhood a long time ago. The negative influence those people have on each other is horrid, those streets eat kids like Trent and his boys ALIVE. I see it every day Ann, everyday".

Trent is a good boy and so are his friends. My son, at the end of junior year has a 3.5 GPA, He made such an impression on his supervisor he lets MY son work as much as he wants. His friends are just like him! HE'S A GOOD BOY!!!! and all of his friends are good boys! and he's all I have. "Austin, the shooting on the beltway, have they identified the body, I need to know please??!!" "Ann please tell me that the criminal resisting arrest,,, do you think it was Trent?"

"Criminal! Resisting arrest! The news said he was shot in the back how is that resisting arrest !!!!" I shout at Austin. "I'll call you as soon as I talk to my captain to find out the kid's name." Austin says coldly. "I'll call you right back Ann." Dial tone. I dropped my phone on the floor and convulse into heart wrenching sobs. Not my son God, please not my SON!!

As I'm praying and sobbing to God on my sofa, I feel four heavy paws walk across my back down my chest into my lap, my forever friend and companion my constant pal, Earl. Earl stares me directly in my eyes as if to say girl you always go all the way to the left, you know that Boy is just fine.

I wish I could feel normal, I wish I didn't have fears, fears a black mother has every time her son walks out that front door. I tried to calm down as my pet Earl, Austin please call, please call!!!! The ringing of my phone makes me jump sending Earl rolling to the floor. It's Omar! "Hey Mama Ann nothing yet, his phone is still going straight to voicemail. "My heart sinks further, "Thanks so much I'll keep you posted and vice versa." I somehow manage to replied. "Sure thing mama Ann."

My phone rings again, Maren from work, hi Maren what's up? Maren my oldest and dearest friend and coworker keeps me filled in on all the gossip when I'm not at the hospital. I don't have time for Maren today I have to keep my phone line clear. "Hey girl, Maren starts, it's been quiet today." I interrupt her. "Hey lady I'm expecting a very important phone call, quick question, Maren anyone come to the ER fitting Trent's description last night? " I blurted out. "Ann did Trent not come home last night? Where did he go? Who is he with?" Maren starts with her arsenal of questions.

"Girl I gotta go I'm waiting on a callback from Austin."

"Since when did you start talking to your brother? My God Ann!!! And the God we serve will never give you beyond what you can bear. He would never do this to you, Trent is fine. He's either passed out somewhere, his phone may be dead, it can be 1001 excuses, don't let the worries dominate your thoughts. I'm praying for you both, I love you please let me know as soon as you hear anything, Maren rambles on. My shift ends in three hours I'll be on my way over to your house then, you will not be alone!" As more tears flow down my face I hang up with my closest dearest friend.

More silence. I look over at my coffee and my third boiled egg and realized I haven't put anything on my stomach and I still cannot. Earl jumps on the sofa next to me, he can feel my pain and stress. Once again... I left my iPad up. I go on social media searching for anything, any ideas, just anything. I search my friends I search my sons' friends nothing still nothing.

Austin please call me!!! Never did I ever think I would be desperately anticipating a call from my brother. I pick up myself, I dial Trent's number again, for the one hundredth time, straight to voicemail. Where are you baby! Please be OK! I drop my phone to the ground as it's ringing an unknown number. Normally I would never answer unknown numbers but today I'm answering everything, hello, hello in desperation I say hello again, no answer, hello, the recorded message about a student loan fills my ears and my heart with emptiness.

I stretch out on the sofa next to Earl and wait. What else is there to do but wait, I have to wait. I must've drifted off to sleep for fifteen minutes, later my phone is ringing, it's Austin! I hastily answer it on the first ring. "Ann.?" The longest pause in history. "The young man who was shot in his back on 395, his name was Sean King. He lives about five blocks from you. It wasn't Trent."

As my stomach loosens and my heart beat slows I breathe THANK YOU God, silently and selfishly I thank God again. But Sean King is someone's baby just not mine. As I'm processing reality Austin is babbling something, I start to listen. Ann, Sean King was a young man who just graduated early from high school who happened to be deaf. He was having car problems and he trusted the police to help him but they failed him and he ended up dead on 395. He was just trying to get home from a job interview and because he was having car problems he was speeding home but ended up dead before he could get there.

I had never heard my brother so bleak and grim, he sounded broken, he sounded defeated, he sounded wounded.

"Just imagine if that was Trent, Austin just imagine." I told him.

"I talked to my captain and a few of my colleagues in other precincts and districts, no description of Trent in any shape or form."

"Dammit and where is he!!" I yelled

"Ann? Only time will tell."

"Austin we are now playing the waiting game. I have to hang up Trent may be calling at any second or news that someone has seen my son. I'll keep you posted and if you hear anything Austin please let me know ASAP."

"I'll call you either way Ann, you're my sister and you and my nephew need me."

I hang up with Austin and continue to wait. As the seconds turn to minutes and the minutes turn to hours I drift in and out of sleep with the television on local news, my tablet right next to me, my phone on my chest as I wait. Someone is knocking at the door thank God he left his key. As I snatch open the door I see Maren my dearest closest friend. I collapse in her arms. Maren collects me and puts me back on my sofa. Earl quickly makes a beeline for my bedroom cause he and Maren have a love-hate relationship.

"Ann I have been calling Trent all afternoon it's going straight to voicemail."

"I know, I know."

"Have you eaten today Ann?"

"How can I eat? I wouldn't be able to hold anything down."

Maren quickly heads to the refrigerator, retrieves a left-over bowl of soup from yesterday then reheats it in the old microwave. "Here eat it." Maren demands placing it in front of me after retrieving it. As I put a spoonful of soup in my mouth the saltiness makes me feel a little better. We stay like this for an hour and a half, me on the sofa and she on the chase lounge and still no Trent.

As 7 PM approaches Maren has to go home. She is the caretaker of her two elderly parents and I know she has to get them settled, fed and ready for bed. We embrace as I walk her to the door. Girl pray that's the final word I'm gonna' say to you. Trent is fine I feel it in my entire spirit. Believe it my friend, Maren says walking through the door. As I close the door Earl appears out of nowhere. Obviously he's hungry so I go to fill his bowl. The phone, in my pocket, signals me of an incoming text alert. Austin has been texting every hour on the hour, all with no updates. There were nine *no updates*, thank you Austin.

I'm still waiting. I slowly get up from my perch to relieve my bladder. I bring my phone, my iPad and my house phone which I never use. As I'm relieving my bladder I hear a faint metallic key sound. Without wiping I jump off the toilet and run to the front door and snatch it open as Trent turns the knob to our front door!!! Hey mommy you alright? Trent ask with the biggest smile and dimples you ever want to see. But his smile soon fades as he's looking into my face. I must've looked like some woman out of a horror movie as I screamed where have you been?!!

Trent quickly gets on the defensive, oblivious to what I have been going through. "Now mommy I told you yesterday while you were at work that I was working a double, my first one, remember. And remember that I told you that Steve said if I keep doing what I'm doing I can get even more overtime.!!! If I keep up the pace I'll have my car before I go back to school Senior year, is going to be lit!!!!". Searching my eyes he still sees my pain, "Mommy my phone died, I didn't have my charger. When I did try calling you it kept going to voicemail. I was calling you from my jobs landline, as well I couldn't text your phone from a landline and when I could get a break to call you your phone kept going to voicemail. You kept bragging about your new life how as soon as you wake up you're going bike riding. I didn't think you didn't know I wasn't home. Mommy what's wrong, aren't you happy for me?" Trent you just don't understand as a whirlwind of tears and sobs come out of my body, you don't know what I've been through I just thought...... I just thought, I couldn't complete my sentence as I hold my son closer and closer, and closer Praying for his tomorrow.

Starseed

by

Morgan Danielle Day

The clock on the stove read 12am. Although it was purposefully set seven minutes early Delicia knew she wouldn't make it to Nelson's Bar and Grill by midnight. She hopped around the living room trying to get her black Giussepe thigh high boots over her shiny black high waisted leggings. 12:03 the clock read. "Damn", Delicia said in a shrill tone. She ran to the hall way mirror, reapplied her Ruby Woo matte red lipstick, puckered her lips and let out a big smack. She turned to the side admiring her pronounced curves, Delicia was a 5'3" knock out. She wore a long wavy Brazilian weave that no one could ever tell didn't belong to her. It complimented her light brown skin and people often mistook her for Dominican or biracial, but she was proudly black mixed with black, no cream, no sugar, just black. Delicia picked up her body bag and bolted out the door.

She slowly pulled up to the lounge, and looked for parking. Ashamed of her silver 2005 Hyundai Elantra hooptie, Delicia didn't want to park too close to Nelson's so that no one could see her leaving the embarrassing automobile. She wanted to look fierce, and her poor car just couldn't match her fly. Delicia desperately longed for a new car but with a modest theatre teacher's salary it just wasn't possible at the moment. Sure, she could get a more stable job but she appreciated her freedom. Delicia was a butterfly and needed to keep her schedule open for her impromptu adventures. It was her first night hanging with Patrick and she needed to appear like she had her shit together. This was Los Angeles. Appearance meant everything in this city, and Delicia was not going to allow her car with a serious dent on the passenger's side to block the possibility of a new relationship and industry networking opportunities.

She pulled out her I phone 7 and searched for Patrick's number. Delicia hadn't yet saved it because she had an aversion for saving numbers of people that she wasn't sure would remain in her life. She dialed Patrick's number. "Hey I'm here. I'm walking up to the door now." Delicia saw a bald brown head pop out of the front door. Patrick was shorter than she usually liked but he had a nice smile and was a hell of a dresser. Tonight he rocked a black leather jacket over a brown Fendi see through shirt, black jeans and black boots with gun metal hardware. They had met at a Halloween party two weeks prior at a mutual friend's house. Patrick had tried to flirt with every female at the event. Delicia didn't usually go for the "look at me" type of dude but she appreciated Patrick's sincerity once he approached her.

They greeted with a church hug. Delicia made sure not to rub too closely against Patrick. Upon entering the dimly lit club there was a bar in the back right corner and a band with all black musicians in the front of the house. In the middle of Nelson's was a lounge area with leather burgundy booths and tables. "I wanna introduce you to my homie Duane," said Patrick. "It's his birthday tonight". Delicia looked at Duane. He was a brown skin, husky, middle aged man, wearing a grey suit and crystal necklaces around his neck. "Hey Duane this is Delicia." "Nice to meet you," said Delicia. Duane stared at her without saying a word. Feeling awkward Delicia decided she'd grab herself a drink. She walked over to the bar. "I've been here fifteen minutes already and this negro hasn't even offered to by me a drink.", she thought. She knew Patrick was definitely not the one.

As Delicia sat down at the bar two ladies came and sat beside her. "Bartender get this girl a drink on me!", said the lady next to Delicia. "Hey I'm Shawna." Shawna was beautiful. She looked like a video vixen with her long hair, light brown skin, hourglass figure and perfectly beat face. Her YSL bag solidified that she was indeed a "bad bitch". Her friend

Andy was also easy on the eyes. She had the looks of a supermodel with her sassy braids, dark chocolate skin and long legs. "Thanks" Delicia said. "No problem", said Shawna. "Our friend Duane sent us over to come get you." "Really? I thought he didn't like me by the way he was just staring at me.", Delicia replied. Shawna and Andy giggled. "He was just trying to figure you out," retorted Andy. "He's a psychic guru, real good peoples". Delicia received her martini. "Come on.", said Shawna. She grabbed Delicia's hand and guided her back to the lounge section where Patrick, Duane and all the other men congregated.

Delicia sat down unsure of what to say or do. Once again she noticed Duane starring at her. She looked away. Eye contact felt dangerous, and her gut didn't know exactly where to place this strange man. Duane began making his way towards Delicia. He quickly sat beside her and began whispering in her ear. "You are an extremely special person. I've never met someone with an aura as bright as yours. It's brighter than anyone here in this club, and you don't even know it yet, but you will. I'm here to help you."

Duane slowly backed away from Delicia's ear and stayed seated beside her. Delicia stunned by this man's boldness and candor was at a loss for words. "Um hi I'm Delicia", she said as she stuck her hand out to shake Duane's. "You've already told me that", Duane said. "You must be a Sag." "What makes you say that", replied Delicia. "Because you like to be free", answered Duane. "Am I right?" "I'm an Aquarius sun with a Sagittarius moon. But yea I like to be free who doesn't?" Responded Delicia. Duane chuckled. "Some people think that's what they want, but you need it. You're a butterfly.", he said. Delicia held her breath wondering how he could possibly know that. "Here take my number", said Duane. Delicia's left eyebrow raised "Is that cool with Patrick?", she questioned. "Naw, it's not like that. You may feel like a butterfly but you're really a Starseed. It's my divine duty to assist my tribe in their spiritual development." Delicia opened her Marc Jacobs bag and grabbed her phone. For some reason Delicia felt the need to save his number. No one in Hollyweird had ever offered her their help before. She somehow knew Duane was well connected despite whether or not she knew if his intentions were completely benevolent.

Delicia looked at her phone ad saw that it was 2:48am. She had an audition the next morning so she knew it was time to leave. Delicia's eyes scoured the club and saw Patrick spitting game to a blond chick. "I'm out" she thought. Delicia exited through the large double doors and made her way towards her car. "Wait Delicia!", Patrick jogged briskly to catch up. "Let me walk you to your car." "Naw, I'm good", replied Delicia. She was nervous. She didn't have any interest in Patrick whatsoever, but she didn't need him seeing her busted vehicle. As far as Delicia was concerned she could still uphold her moniker of "bad bitch". It was best to let him think that he messed up instead of

Delicia revealing her shortcomings. Patrick accepted defeat and walked back towards the club. Entering her car Delicia let out a huge sigh. She drove home.

The next day Delicia woke up in a panic. The home screen of her cell phone read 9:08am. She had snoozed through her alarm several times and her audition was at 10am. Delicia quickly jumped out of bed, and brushed her hair and teeth. Thank God she had chosen her outfit the night before or else leaving would have been impossible. She slipped on a red sheath dress, applied eye liner and mascara, dabbed her lips with her nude Fenty lip gloss and headed for the door. "Why am I always on CP time?", she kept chanting to herself. She was definitely paying the price for partying all night. Delicia arrived on the Paramount studio lot. She gave her information to the burly Latino guard at the gate and searched for parking. Parking was a nightmare! Paramount was regal with grandiose movie posters adorning the entire lot. It was the visual culmination of how Delicia imagined living her life. She wanted to wake up every day and head to set to film, but not just any set. She wanted to work on a lot that felt like a palace grand enough for a butterfly to roam freely. Finally! Someone pulled out of a spot and Delicia took it with a flash. Running up to the audition room in her five-inch black stilettos her cell phone read 10:13am. "Please let me audition. Please let me audition.", she chanted. Delicia opened the giant stark white doors. There were at least thirty women in the waiting room that could have passed for her douplegangers. They were Delicia's exact type. Height, complexion, size, all of these women who looked just like her were her competition. This role would simply come down to who the casting director was familiar with, and who nailed the audition.

Delicia signed in. She was definitely going to be able to audition. Casting was running behind as per usual. She sat down, pulled out her audition sides and went over her lines over and over again. She waited a total of one hour and forty-two minute before her name was called. Delicia gathered her things and entered the room with confidence and grace. She knew she was going to be a forced to be reckoned with despite the other wannabe Delicia's vying for the same part. Upon entering Delicia's jaw dropped. There, in the middle of the casting director's table sat Duane. The same Duane she had met the night before at Nelson's Bar and Grill. He wore a white t-shirt with blue jeans and the same crystal necklaces he had on the night before. This shook Delicia. She then questioned her every move from last night. "Was I rude to him? Why didn't I say more?, Does he remember me?" Delicia made eye contact with Duane. She felt the danger of his gaze in her gut. "Whenever you're ready.", said Duane in a cavalier manner. Delicia began speaking and then stopped herself. "Can I start over?", she asked. Duane nodded his head. She began the scene again and to her surprised gave a flawless delivery. "Well done", said Duane. Delicia smiled. "I told you

you were special." Not knowing how to respond Delicia said "Thank you so much for your time" and exited the room.

Walking back to her car Delicia was overcome with a rush of excitement. She looked down at her phone to see a text message from Duane. "Good job Starseed. Call me at 6pm." This was the second time Duane had referred to her as a Starseed. Delicia decided to look up what it meant exactly. Urbandictionary.com defined Starseed as: A person who is spiritually aware, having a strong connection to the divine creator. Starseeds are said to be **old soul**s sent back to earth to transform the world into the **heaven on earth** predicted after the end of times. Such persons may display spiritual gifts of **clairvoyance**. Being able to read minds, other's emotions or see future events." A chill ran up Delicia's spine. She was a very spiritual person, but regretfully allowed the superficiality of Hollyweird to distract her from her connection with God. She sat in the Paramount parking lot pondering the definition for another thirty minutes then drove off.

Delicia grabbed her cell phone as she sat in her lavender bubble bath. The screen read 5:55pm. She had anxiously been waiting to call Duane all day and just couldn't hold off another second. She nervously dialed his number. Duane picked up before the first ring could even finish. "Starseed", he said. "Hi Duane how are you?", replied Delicia with a grin. "I'm well. What are you doing tonight?", Duane asked. Delicia didn't want the opportunity to meet with him to slip through her perfectly manicured fingertips so she blurted "I'm free" without reluctancy. "Great! I'll text you my address, meet me here as soon as you can." Duane hung up the phone.

"Damn", Delicia thought. "Time to get cute". She didn't want to appear as if she were trying too hard so she put on some figure-hugging grey jeans, a white cut off t-shirt with a Prada logo and some black booties with a silver zipper up the front. Duane's spot was forty minutes away from Delicia's apartment in North Hollywood. Upon pulling up to his gate Delicia made sure to park around the corner so he couldn't see her eye soar of a car from the window. She noticed all of the colorful flowers and fruit trees that framed Duane's sophisticated Ranch style home. Duane opened his wood and stained-glass front door wearing a light grey sweatsuit. "Glad you could make it" he said to Delicia with a giant grin across his face. Duane grabbed Delicia's hand and escorted her inside of his home.

Duane's living room looked like a Buddhist temple exploded all over it. There were Tibetan singing bowls for every chakra, yoga matts, plants, and large crystals accompanied by the smell of sandalwood incense. "So I hear you're a healer.", Delicia said. "I can definitely feel the positive energy in your space it's very peaceful." Delicia wasn't sure why but she felt safe. A strong sense of relaxation entered her body. "Please take off your shoes.", Duane commanded politely. He grabbed a bundle of sage and slowly waved the herbs in front of Delicia's body. Delicia respected the ritual and felt the need to remain silent. "Good job today Starseed. You're a hell of an actress, but you have work to do spiritually. I want you to have the role of Patricia, but she is fairly advanced in her spirituality and nuanced in the art of seduction. Think of Dorothy Dandridge as Carmen with the swag of Erykah Badu. When is the last time you've had a healing?"

Delicia didn't know how to respond. She had never had a healing of any kind. She was typically the go to person for all of her friends to bombard with their problems. No one ever listened to hers. On second thought, no one really cared to ever ask. Delicia was close with her family but her older sister Zena had always been the problem child, and as the saying goes: "The squeaky wheel gets the oil." As beautiful and kind as Delicia was she was still background material to her parents. "I've never had one before.", she replied. "What kind of healer are you Duane?",she asked. Duane smiled. "I do sound baths, reiki, tantric, crystal, herbal, you name it I do it, but I think we'll start with a reiki session for you. We have to raise your vibration if you're going to fulfill your humanitarian duties as a Starseed." Duane pulled out a black massage table from his hall way closet and unfolded it. "Lie down on your back.", he said. Delicia carefully climbed on the table and closed her eyes. Duane put a Carnelian crystal on Delicia's sacral chakra and an Amethyst above her head. Delicia fell into a deep sleep as

Duane began waving his hands over her body never once touching her. She could feel the magnitude of his energy permeate her aura. It felt trustworthy, but most importantly it felt safe. Duane touched Delicia's shoulder ever so gently to let her know the session was over. "How do you feel?", he asked. Delicia didn't move. She couldn't. Words couldn't describe how to explain the sensation she was experiencing. The energy was so overwhelming that she began crying. Duane was familiar with this type of catharsis. He allowed her feel exactly what she needed in the moment. "Thank you" Delicia whimpered through snot and runny mascara. Duane bowed and helped Delicia off of the massage table. "When I get back from Atlanta we will finish your healing."

Delicia left with a heightened sense of gratitude. Someone cared about her. Someone cared about her development as a human being and her career as an actress. She turned her pandora to the Erykah Badu station and drove home. The next morning Delicia woke up to a phone call from her agent Melissa from CSED Talent Agency. Melissa informed Delicia that she was being considered for the role of Patrica in the CW's new show "Catastrophic". Delicia jumped for joy! She hopped out of bed and began a twerk celebration dance. She then abruptly stopped in her tracks. "I'm supposed to be on a new journey towards spiritual enlightenment. I don't need to be shaking my ass." For a second she thought about calling Duane but she knew he would already know. Delicia called her mother instead. The phone rang three times then her mother answered. "Ma guess what!?", Delicia said with delight. "I'm up for a huge role on a new CW show." "Wait a minute baby.", her mother quickly cut her off. "That's your sister on the other line. I need to make sure she's ok. She gets out of rehab today. I'll call you right back." Click. Mom hung up the phone. Delicia was hurt but definitely not surprised. This was the norm in the Leggum family.

Duane was set to return on Saturday. Delicia found it hard to think of anything other than seeing Duane and her callback for the next three days, but managed to the meditate and pray in the mornings and evenings. This was a big step for her. Delicia felt proud that she was doing her due diligence in forming a deeper connection with her spirituality. Finally Saturday came. The callback for "Catastrophic" was on Monday. Delicia had a plethora of questions to bombard Duane with when she saw him. Ring ring ring, it was Duane calling. "Hello Duane", Delicia answered. "Starseed, meet me at my house at 11:11 tonight." He hung up before Delicia could ask any questions, but she was definitely going to be there. This time she knew exactly what to wear. There was no need for heels and heavy makeup. Healings didn't require that. She wanted to arrive on time so she meditated and left early. Delicia knocked on the wood and stained- glass door at exactly 11:11pm. Duane answered. "Good job. You're on time." Of course, Delicia replied. "We have a lot of work to do.", Duane said as he walked Delicia to his in-home studio. Delicia hadn't seen the studio last time so this excited her. "Would you like something to drink.", Duane asked. "I have water, apple juice and Cabernet." She didn't know if this was a test so she chose water. "I'll bring the wine in the studio just in case you change your mind." he said.   Duane opened the doors to his studio and sitting on a couch inside was Patrick. Delicia's eyes widened. This made her slightly uncomfortable but she brushed it off. After all she was in good hands with Duane. Patrick grinned and slowly looked Delicia up and down. He stood up from the couch and greeted her with a hug.

"I didn't know there would be anyone else here tonight.", complained Delicia. "I know you and Patrick are acquainted so I felt it wouldn't be an issue.", Duane explained. "Now, we worked on raising your vibration last time you were here. I'm guessing you've been seeing angel numbers like 222, 333, or 555. This is because you are in alignment." This impressed Delicia as she thought seeing those patterns was pure coincidence. "The character of Patricia is spiritually aligned so you must be too, but she also has that raw sex appeal of Dorothy Dandridge in Carmen. You have it but you need to be more unapologetic in the ownership of your womanhood." "I guess I can understand what you mean by that.", said Delicia. "Now I know you know Patrick. Seduce him." "Excuse me?", Delicia asked with confusion. "It's acting of course", Duane explained. "Go up to him and make him want you without saying anything. Delicia felt stuck. She knew this would help her solidify the role but she was uneasy. Delicia walked over to Patrick, sat next to him, crossed her legs in his direction and put her hand gracefully on his thigh then looked at Duane for approval. Duane and Patrick both broke out into a condescending laughter. "Is that it?", asked Duane. "Delicia make him want you.", he scolded. "Sit on his lap, and kiss his neck." "What, is that necessary?", Delicia debated. Duane rolled his eyes and responded. "Because if you can't do that here how are you going to be able to do it on set with an entire crew and whoever else watching? Delicia sat on Patrick's lap and gave him a peck on the cheek. "Really kiss him Starseed.", Duane commanded." Take your time and use your tongue." "Okay, I'm uncomfortable." Delicia said and then got up from Patrick's lap. "Here". Duane poured a glass of Cabernet and handed it to her. Delicia took a big gulp. "Patrick help her out." Patrick grabbed Delicia's arm and sat her back down on his lap. He grabbed her by the waste and begin kissing her aggressively. He slid his hand underneath Delicia's sports bra, and she jumped up. "I thought this was acting!" She yelled. "Art imitates life.", Duane responded. Delicia wanted to leave. Is this really what she had to do for the part? "I'm not comfortable with Patrick." She explained. Duane sighed and told Patrick to leave. "You need a tantric healing. It's going to help redirect some of your guarded sexual energy." Delicia was relieved. She could use a healing after what just transpired. "Take off your clothes." Duane commanded. "For a healing?", Delicia said with terror and confusion. "Yes we're going to have intercourse so I can heal you. It's required of a tantric healing." Duane approached Delicia, grabbed her throat and licked her cheek. "I don't want it, I don't want it!", Delicia screamed and pulled away. "Get out! It's obvious you are not a Starseed.", Duane yelled. Delicia ran out of the house with lightning speed. She sat in her car and broke down crying.

The next day Delicia received a text message from Melissa, her agent. She had been dropped, but Delicia felt righteous. She was a butterfly and would eventually land where she needed. If selling her soul was the only way to procure a role on television she didn't want it. If Duane had taught her anything it was the power of meditation and forming a deeper connection with God. With a solid foundation in her faith Delicia could combat anything that came her way, that included a less than involved family and insidious industry vampires out to take advantage of young women. She looked at the clock. It read 1:11. Delicia was proud. She was indeed in alignment.

My World Implodes

by

R.C. McDonald

I woke up to the sounds of Police sirens one cold and windy day in November 1991. Living in a small town just south of Chicago these sounds were somewhat rare. It wasn't like the big city, we didn't have lots of crime and most people minded their own business.

I lived in a cottage style home in the North part of town we called Valley Park. Residents of Valley Park worked hard for a living, mostly in professional jobs. It was a town of strong Catholic families with parents pushing their children to follow in their professional and religious footsteps.

Over time the sirens got louder then suddenly stopped. Still dragging myself out of bed I hear a loud bang at the front door. I didn't think much of it I just put on my robe and headed for the door. My bedroom was located on the top floor so before I could get to the door an even harder knock was heard. The knocks got louder and more intense, so much more that my twenty-year old son, Phillip, came running from his room.

Before the two of us managed to make our way to the door it violently opens. Three Police officers charged in; guns drawn. After a quick look at the first floor they spot us on the steps then demanded us to stop.

We stopped, but not before one of the three Officers charges Phillip, knocking him down the steps with a gun pointed at his head. Phillip, a somewhat reserved person, didn't resist as they forced handcuffs on his muscular wrist.

"What's going on, leave him alone." I screamed.

"What's your name?" The first Officer yelled as Phillip lay quietly on the steps.

"Phillip, Phillip Mackenzie." He struggled to say.

"Phillip Mackenzie, you're under arrest for the murder of a Miss. Martha Harper." One Officer stated as the other two drag Phillip to his feet.

"I didn't murder nobody."

"My son is not a murderer." I screamed.

Ignoring our comments Phillip is dragged out of the door and into an awaiting patrol car with what seem to be the entire neighborhood watching. It was quite embarrassing.

Nothing like this has ever happened to anyone in my family or to anyone in the neighborhood. I cried and screamed as they pulled away with my youngest child.

I was a widow of just five months when the incident occurred. My husband recently dying in a controversial war. Together we had two children, Mya who at the time was 22, a college senior at a nearby Christian University and Phillip.

When Phillip entered kindergarten, he was never able to keep up with the class. He always seem to lag behind the other kids though he paid attention. At times the teacher said it appeared Phillip mostly drifted into space and was not really paying attention to the class. She wanted to send him to a county school for retarded children.

I complained to the Principle and counselors but they ultimately agreed with the teacher. Against my wishes they began the paperwork to have Phillip transferred, I was devastated. How could the school just take a kid and treat him like he was nothing, they didn't even test him, they didn't even talk to him, they had no idea who he was, they were just plain old mean.

There was no way in Hell I was going to let them label my child like that ruining him for life. I left those sons of a bitches and angrily marched down to the School Board's building and demanded that the receptionist let me speak with the Commissioner. She so politely told me that the Commissioner was in a meeting and wasn't expected to finish for another four hours. That didn't bother me; I sat in the chair next to the receptionist desk and waited. I had waited for over five hours when Commissioner Pursy walked toward the empty receptionist desk since she had left one-hour prior. Good evening, I said stopping the tall slender hairy Commissioner. He looked confused; I beg your pardon he replied "Why are you here?" He continued.

I explained the situation to Commissioner Pursy asking for his help. Eager to leave he expressed his sympathy but stated there was nothing he could do. I did not accept that as an answer. Realizing he didn't care and was in a rush to leave I blocked him from making any progress toward the door. Noticing my aggressive attitude a nearby security guard walks toward me and began pulling me away from the Commissioner, allowing him to leave the building.

An hour later I arrived home to my husband and Phillip playing a memory game. My husband Ted had been home from his Military duties for several weeks but was about to deploy over sees the first of the month. He spent lots of time with Phillip, teaching him his letters, numbers and world history. Ted loved history and looked for any opportunity to talk just anything historical.

Phillip could repeat the alphabet forward and backward; counting to 100 was no problem; recognizing every color in a box of 50 crayons was a snap. But when it came to writing and reading, he regularly confused numbers and letters. It made me think about a news story I saw several years earlier. It delt with kids who were very smart but had a hard time reading and writing. I couldn't remember why the story was on the news I just knew that I had to find out.

I told my husband that I was going to the local news station and would return. Once I arrived, I was greeted by a young intern.

"Hello, how my I help you?" He asked so politely with unexpected emergency for eight o'clock at night.

"Hi, I would like to speak to someone about a story I saw on your news station about two years ago."

"Sure, I will have someone from research help you."

"Thank you young man."

"No problem."

The young boy walked to a back room and returned several minutes later with a young reporter I had seen on the nightly news many times. She took me into a room with several micro-film machines. I explained to her what I was looking for and she instantly knew where to look.

That next day I approached the school's principle to insist he have Phillip tested as were the children in the news story. Principle Fitzpatrick denied the request. Refusing to accept no as an answer I stayed in his office pacing until he caved. He scheduled the test for the next day.

Phillip was diagnosed with a learning disability identified as Dyslexia. On the surface he was fine, as a matter of fact he tested in the ten percentiles in aptitude. Together the school, myself and my husband decided that Phillip would benefit from a newly developed program for children with Dyslexia. The program was run out of a neighboring school which was more equipped to teach students with the disability.

Now here we are fourteen years later. Phillip having graduated from high school with honors now attending the University of Chicago majoring in Biology. He has plans of becoming a doctor with the intent of helping others with the same disability. Phillip is out-going; member of the school's Students with Disabilities club; Captain of the local Volleyball team; Actor in the town's theatre. He has thrived even with the death of his father.

With all his accomplishments being a murderer is not one of them. I cried so hard when that Patrol car drove away and turned the corner. I waited for one of my neighbors to comfort me, but that didn't happen, they retreated into their homes leaving me to suffer alone.

It was now 8:00 am, some two hours after Phillip was taken from home. As I paced back and forth at the Police station for over an hour I wondered if I would ever see my son again.

My daughter drove down from school and joined me. Together we waited until noon before someone called us back.

We were taken into a large room with a glass window separating the room into halves. It looked to be the typical prisoner/visitation room like on tv, where the visitors sit on one side and the prisoners sit on the other side. The Guard pointed us to Phillip at the far-right side of the room. I began crying.

"Mom" Phillip said as I sat down.

"Don't cry." He continued.

"Phillip what happened?" My daughter asked bluntly.

"They said I killed somebody."

"You didn't do that did you?" She continued.

"Mya, of course he didn't." I replied.

"No, no I didn't kill her."

"Who was this woman. Did you know her?" I asked.

"Yeah, she was one of the other actors at the theatre."

"Why do they think you killed her." Mya asked.

"They said somebody said they saw me kill her."

"Who in the hell said that!" I said yelling.

"I don't know. They won't tell me."

"We need to get to the bottom of this. I'm going to fight this." I yelled even louder.

"Mother, please not so loud." Mya insisted.

"This is my son and I'm going to get him out of this place."

Later that evening I was exhausted from calling over ten lawyers. I was not familiar with the law, its nuances and all its greed. It seems as though every lawyer I spoke with was only after my money. I'm not a rich woman, I'm simply a widowed

Office Manager. I couldn't afford the fees those greedy ambulance chasers wanted. I even contacted the Veterans Administration for legal help and was denied due to my son's age.

After two long days of searching for a lawyer I realized that the best person to represent Phillip was me. I was the only person who had his well-being in mind. This was personal, this was the only way of giving my son the best chance of beating these charges.

After assigning myself to the case I met with Phillip to learn about his relationship with Miss. Martha Harper. He explained to me that she had just recently joined the theatre group. Apparently, she was a new comer to Valley Park, having just moved here from out west. She wasn't the worse actress but she wasn't the best either, he explained. Phillip couldn't tell me much more than that as they rarely spoke.

That next day I met with a Mr. Harold Star, the witness, a neighbor of Ms. Harper and himself a member of the theatre. We met at his home, a small Cape Cod sitting directly across from the victim's home. Mr. Star is a tall husky man covered in facial hair that complemented the thinning capitulum hair.

"Mrs. Anderson, come in please." Mr. Star said as he opened the door to his home.

"Thank you." I replied as I walked comfortably through the door and into the sparsely furnished Livingroom. Before sitting Mr. Rover, the Prosecuting Attorney, walked in from the outdated kitchen. I had never met him before that day but I had seen him at the Preliminary Hearing.

"Mr. Rover, thanks for allowing me to meet with Mr. Star." I said.

"Mrs. Anderson, why should I care that you are meeting with Mr. Star. You are not a lawyer and have never been trained in law Enforcement."

"Are you trying to say that I don't know what I'm doing?"

"Hey if the shoe fits." He said sarcastically.

"Mr. Star." I said ignoring the comment.

"I appreciate you taking the time to meet with me." I continue as the two men take seats at opposite sides of the room.

"So, you think you saw the accused on the day Ms. Harper was murdered."

"First of all, I know that you are Phillip's mother. I feel that you don't believe that he was at Martha's house the day of the murder or any day. But you obviously don't know your son."

"Wait a minute. I know my son." I defended.

"Oh, so I guess you know that he has been sleeping with Martha and two other women of the theatre. Your son is a playboy. He uses women."

"You're lying." I yelled.

"Oh yeah, and did he tell you that he got one of them

pregnant?"

"What the hell?" I said shocked.

"Go talk to your son. I believe he killed her. He killed her cause she was the one pregnant and she threated to tell the other women when she found out about them."

I left the house defeated. I couldn't believe a word Mr. Star was saying but I was too pissed to confront Phillip.

Later that night I opened the case folder as I had every night since I took on the role of lawyer. I thought I had analyzed the entire case but apparently I failed to do so. I don't know why I overlooked the autopsy report, I guess I didn't think it was important enough. When I read the report, something jumped out at me giving some credence to Mr. Star's comments about the victim. When I read that she was a twenty-seven-year-old woman who was about fifteen weeks pregnant my heart dropped. I didn't know what to make of this I just knew Phillip did not impregnate that woman.

I wanted the truth. Though it was well past visiting hours I headed to that jail to see Phillip. I was given hell for attempting to speak with him at such a late hour but they gave me an exception considering I served as his lawyer. I found it hard to relax as I waited in the visitor area my heart ponding so fast I knew it was just a few minutes away from exploding.

When Phillip finally arrived, my motherly instincts took over along with a side dish of anger. "Did you get that woman pregnant?" I yelled. Phillip was shocked. He didn't know what to say so he kept quiet.

"That woman was pregnant, did you get her pregnant?"

"I don't know. She said I did."

"You told me you didn't know her."

Phillip stood up then walked back to the awaiting Guard.

&

Phillip and I had not spoken since that day, some two months ago. Many times I tried to put on my lawyer's hat to visit my client but my mother's hat kept getting in the way.

I knew I couldn't handle the case since I had no trust in my own son. In defeat, I called the county and got him a public defender. In my heart I knew he was guilty so I hoped that Mr. Carroll, the public defender, could somehow get him off.

I left Valley Park to live in a town some twenty miles away. I just didn't want to know all the secrets my son was keeping. Phillip and I were close, at least I thought we were. We did a lot together, he had plans for the future and I just knew he rarely dated.

My daughter visited regularly trying to get me to visit Phillip, but I refused. On her last visit she got so mad she vowed never to visit me again if I didn't support Phillip.

I had hope when 1990 rang in, but this whole thing made me re-think my entire life. I let my daughter walk away with no intention of ever seeing her or Phillip again.

Time past, my best friends had become Colt 45 and Old Granddad. We spent lots of time together, at least half of every day. When we weren't together, I was lying flat on the air mattress of the studio apartment.

While much of the time was spent forgetting the past somehow the past stayed with the present. Unfortunately the closer the trial the more I drank. The more I drank the more I wanted to die.

Easter that year was tough to get through. From the moment I woke up to the time I was ready to lay my head down for the night I drank. I was determined to end it all by drinking but I kept waking up. Didn't make any since why I was still walking the Earth it was just how it was. Even with mixing sleeping pills with the alcohol I still found myself alive.

Apparently my time on Earth was not over. No matter what I did I kept waking up. It was just not meant for me to leave at this time. Though I grew up in a strong Catholic family that attended church several times a week I always thought of myself as just going along for the ride. I always doubted my beliefs, yet whether I realized it or not, I lived the strict Catholic life of my parents; I married a strict Catholic; I was a virgin until I married; I never used artificial means of birth control; My life was my family.

My life was the son and daughter I walked away from because of the shame I felt Phillip's actions caused. A true

Catholic would never turn their back on the ones they love. Like that great being looking out for me I needed to return to Valley Park to look out for Phillip. No matter what mistakes he made Phillip was still my child.

That next day I packed up my stuff, what little I had and headed back to Valley Park. It was exciting seeing the house for the first time in several months, it brought back so many memories.

But I didn't stay long, I had to make my way to the courthouse for the trial. It seemed like forever to get there but in actuality it only took twenty minutes. When I walked into the courthouse Phillip was on the stand being questioned by the Prosecuting Attorney. He noticed me, then stopped before continuing.

"Mr. Anderson, please answer the question." The Prosecuting Attorney requested.

"Yes sir." Phillip said as I sat down.

"Sir, Ms. Harper and I were really good friends. I welcomed her to the area and tried my best to make sure she had everything she needed to be comfortable. I took her to a couple of job interviews; I took her on the tour of Valley Park and helped her whenever she needed something."

As Phillip spoke I realized that he was the son I thought I raised. He was no murderer or womanizer he was a good kid. I relaxed and listened.

"So you knew where she lived."

"Oh, yes sir I did."

"And were you at Ms. Harper's home on the afternoon of the murder?"

"Yes, Ms. Harper needed some groceries so I took some items over to her."

"And why couldn't she get her own groceries, she was in possession of an automobile, correct?"

"Yes sir, but the car was not working and she couldn't afford to fix it until she got paid."

"So why didn't she call somebody else?"

"I'm not quite sure? We got along so I guess she would ask me."

"Well weren't you two sexually involved?"

"Your honor, I object." Phillip's Attorney stated.

"Your honor my question is necessary for further questioning."

"Objection overruled." The Judge replied.

"Young man, please answer the question." The Judge said.

"Sir, Ms. Harper and I did not have a sexual relationship and we never had sex."

"Oh, but according to the witnesses you were the father of her unborn child."

"Sir, she said that but that is not physically possible."

"So you're saying you and the victim never engaged in sexual intercourse."

"That is correct." Phillip replied.

I was so proud of him. My son, he was the son I thought I had. He handled the questions like a gentleman and with confidence. It upsets me that I didn't believe the son I gave birth to twenty-one years to the day.

The Prosecutor continued trying to break Phillip, but he was unbreakable. And why was he unbreakable, because he was telling the truth. Flustered the Prosecutor rest his case.

"Mr. Harris you may cross examine the Defendant?" The Judge announced.

"Yes, your honor." Mr. Harris said standing.

"Mr. Anderson, were you involved with any women at the theatre?" Mr. Harris asked.

"No sir, just friends?"

"Thank you, you are excused."

Phillip takes a seat next to that of Mr. Harris who remains standing.

"Your honor, I would like to call to the stand Ms. Rachel Donaldson." Mr. Harris stated.

"Ms. Donaldson. Please take the stand." The Judge said before a beautiful young woman, no more than twenty years-old walked to the Bailer, who swears her in.

"Ms. Donaldson, do you know the defendant?" Mr. Harris asked.

"Yes, we are both members of the theatre."

"And how long have you known him?"

"For about three years now."

"Did Mr. Anderson ever approach you in a romantic manner."

"No, we went out for soda with others maybe once or twice but that was it."

"Ok, what about other women. Are you aware of him dating any of the other women at the theatre?"

"No, not that I was aware of?"

"Were there any rumors of him dating anyone at the theatre."

"Just from Jonathan Smith."

"Jonathan Smith?"

"Yes he's Harold Star's nephew. He joined the theatre about a year ago."

"So, why would he make such accusations?"

"I don't know, he had just started saying that about a week before the murder."

"Ms. Donaldson, thank you. You are excused."

Mr. Harris requested the Judge grant a two-day recess; which was granted before the court began to empty. As the guards slowly walked Phillip down the aisle toward the court doors, he asked them to stop when they approached me. Surprisingly they agreed.

Phillip walked to me then gave me a long tight hug. "I love you Mom, I knew you would be here." He said as he looked into my eyes.

"I'm so sorry. I let you down." I cried.

"No, no you didn't. You did me a favor. I couldn't stand seeing you worry about me. I know that I didn't murder Ms. Harper but I knew the eye witness had pointed at me. I knew you would not have been able to handle it so when you left it gave me an opportunity to work with Mr. Harris. Thank you so much for being there for me. I will be home soon."

Phillip had endured three months in jail for a crime he didn't commit and was handling it better than the woman who was always supposed to be on his side. I was the one that grew during that time, Phillip was already mature enough to handle life's setbacks and that's what it turned out to be.

Phillip was acquitted of all charges when it was revealed that Mr. Star lied about Phillips relationship with the victim to protect his nephew Jonathan Smith. Mr. Smith killed Ms. Harper in a fit of rage because of the baby she was carrying for him. He insisted that she terminate the pregnancy; She refused. Mr. Smith was sentenced to life in prison for First degree murder.

My relationship with Phillip and my daughter took off like there was never a separation. Though my daughter attends school in Chicago the three of us meet for lunch every Saturday. Apparently Phillip was allowed to keep up his studies while in jail and as a proud Mom I am glad to say that he earned a 4.0 average that semester, my boy.

R.C. McDonald

(Renee)

Renee grew up in the city of Baltimore to a family of four boys, herself, parents and an extended family. She attended the Baltimore City public Schools, having graduated from Forest Park High school. Later she attended Morgan State University where she graduated with a B.S. in Mathematics then one year later a B.S. in Computer Science. She went on to earn a M.S. in Computer Science from Bowie State University and an MBA from the University of Maryland. She has enjoyed working in the technical field for several government agencies including NASA.

Renee's love for writing began as a child. She would write short stories in her spare time but never tried to pursue writing more seriously. As an adult she began taking writing a bit more seriously as she managed to complete her first book. Again, she had no intentions of doing anything with the book but with the encouragement of friends and family she researched the best methods to publishing the book and followed through. Renee enjoys the publishing industry so much she has recently started her own publishing company, Nicholson & fisher. The company is currently in the infancy stage but Renee has set goals for growing the business.

Renee is currently working on several novels, an historical fiction based on Complex Puzzle book, an Anthology of short stories of strong female characters and the beginnings of a Mystery series. Ms. McDonald loves to write historical fictions with strong female characters and plans on publishing her second books by the end of 2020.

Renee works many hours tutoring children in Math and the sciences as she believes the kids are the future. As she wrote Complex Puzzle, Renee realized that all kids, despite their living conditions as a child, can succeed as adults. This philosophy and her love for history are the basis for all her work.

Contributing Authors

Jacquelyn S. Camper (Jackie)

M. Wanda Day Camper

Morgan Danielle Day

Kendra Grace

Alise Naomi-Ann McDonald

Floretta Sharpless

Heather Tate

Jacquelyn S. Camper (Jackie)

Jacquelyn S. Camper (Jackie) currently resides in the Maryland area and is a native of North Carolina. Jackie has old fashion values and believes that everyone should have a chance to express themselves. She promotes education and has achieved both a Bachelor's and Master's degree in Criminal Justice, along with a Master's degree in Education.

Jackie, as friends and family call her, is in the Behavior Health field and believes that everyone should be given quality care in all areas of health regardless of one's social economic status, race, age, etc.

Jackie loves taking long walks and drives with her husband Mike as well as spending quality time with her family and close friends. She constantly engages in storytelling, where she is mostly the one telling the stories of the past and present day. She enjoys listening to soft music mostly Jazz. Jackie has a passion for mankind and will insert herself into their lives to help them with having a better quality of life.

M. Wanda Day Camper

Wanda was raised in Fort Meade and Baltimore, Maryland by way of Fort Jackson, South Carolina. M. Wanda Camper is a loving mother, wife, community advocate, newfound author and gospel choir member. She has been referred to as having the "voice of an angel".

Wanda has a background in banking and human resources and customer service. A graduate of the University of Baltimore with a bachelor's degree in Business Administration, Wanda has shared her business acumen and talent for numbers as an associate with Verizon Wireless for the last 14 years.

Wanda has recently found a new calling to be closer with the Lord and has begun her studies towards a Bachelor of Biblical studies from the North Carolina College of Theology. Having been a featured speaker at a women's empowerment event she is thrilled to share this short story based on her real-life personal experience. It is a cautionary tale of a traumatic time in her life and serves as a release of all the ghost that have held tender emotions captive.

Morgan Danielle Day

Morgan Danielle Day is an actress, dancer, writer/poet and director based in Los Angeles. She grew up in Baltimore, MD where she graduated from The Baltimore School for the Arts with a concentration in theatre performance. She continued her studies at Marymount Manhattan College in New York City, earning a Bachelor of Fine Arts Degree in Theatre.

Morgan has performed in many plays including *The Hendrix Project* directed by Roger Guinevere Smith at The Public Theatre in New York, and has taught acting and dance to students K-12. She made her international debut at the Edinburgh Fringe Festival in Scotland playing the lead role of "Betty" in *Gunshot Medley.* Morgan graduated with her Master of Fine Arts in acting from the California Institute of the Arts and signed with AB2 talent Agency She has since joined the cast of Boney M directed by Edgar Arceneaux where they made their international debut in Lagos Nigeria. Morgan does voice-over looping for series such as *Blackish, Grownish, Modern Family* and *AP Bio. She* recently stared in the independent film *The Council* which will be screened at the 2020 San Diego Black Film Festival, San Francisco Black Film Festival, Las Vegas Black Film Festival, and Charlotte Black Film Festival.

Kendra Grace

Kendra Grace was born and raised in Baltimore, MD. She is the mother of two sons and is the co-business owner of Shear Faith Salon, located in Owings Mills, MD. She is driven by Her love for God, family and the fulfillment of her PURPOSE in life.

Kendra is committed to being authentic and consistently displaying God's love. Her mission is to BE as He's designed, make a difference in people's lives, and encourage others to do the same.

Alise Naomi-Ann McDonald

Alise Naomi-Ann McDonald was born and raised in Baltimore, MD. She attended Towson State University where she majored in Exercise Science. As a student Alise was an all-around gymnast for Towson's Division I gymnastics team.

Alise is an avid reader whose spends most of her free time reading novels. When she manages to put the novels down Alise loves baking and gardening.

Alise works as a Cardiac Sonographer who is preparing to apply to graduate school. She hopes to continue her medical training by entering one of several programs.

Floretta Sharpless

Floretta Sharpless is a native of North Carolina and currently resides in the Maryland area. She is energetic and loves spending time with family and close friends. Floretta thrives on encouraging people around her to reach for their goals. She believes in education and has over her lifetime managed to obtain a Bachelor's degree in Accounting, a Master's degree in Administrative Management and an MBA with a concentration in Information Security Management.

Floretta is a Risk Management Executive who believes that security from both a physical and psychological standpoint is vital. Floretta loves meeting people and manages to make everyone around her feel comfortable enough to be their true selves. Writing and storytelling is one of Floretta's favorite past times. She loves all types of music, but finds herself listening to gospel, which encourages her to ignite her poetic side; as she is a poetic person, who love writing spiritual poetry.

Heather Tate

   Heather Tate was born and raised in Brooklyn, NY. She grew up with a fascination and love of hair upon moving to Baltimore, MD in 1989. As Heather's curiosity and talents in hair grew it clearly became obvious that she had the "Gift" of haircare and styling.

   After graduating from high school Heather immediately enrolled in Ron Thomas School of Cosmetology, excelling in all aspects of hair. Armed with a license, a warm personality, a skill for easy listening and having a team player persona Heather was hired in my first Salon @19 years of age. She enjoyed working with Regis® Salon from 1994-1996 where she excelled in chemical relaxers, coloring, cutting and styling.

In 1996, Heather took a scary yet rewarding chance in going into business for herself. She loved working independently at the successful salon she called W&W hair salon. As a salon owner she learned a great deal about the business of running a business along with increasing her already high level of skills in haircare and customization for individual clients.

From there, Heather started a long-term career of 18 years with JC Penny Salons. It was there where Heather became certified in Mizani®, Redkin®, Matrix®, Paul Mitchell®, Avlon®, and Chi®. Heather's extended career with the nation-wide chain helped her learn teamwork, the latest haircutting, coloring and styling techniques while earning the title of Master Stylist.

With 20 years in the industry Heather stepped out on FAITH to pursue a DREAM of Salon ownership with her best friend and now partner Kendra Grace. The two ladies, sisters by different parents, have opened Shear Faith Salon in Owings Mills MD. The two ladies are enjoying the freedom and sometimes frustrating task of owning such a fine establishment. Heather is like a sister, daughter, mother to all her clients as she has a heart of goal and cares for each of them.

In 2000 Heather married the love of her life. Together they have a beautiful, energetic and well-rounded daughter Autumn. The family currently resides in Baltimore MD with their two cats and the person Heather loves the most, her mom, not far away.